D1138406

STORIES FOR NINE-Y

This entertaining anthology of stories is bound to capture the imagination of the nine-year-olds it was created for. As their horizons broaden beyond their immediate surroundings, children of this age are keen to discover other people's experiences and to share their trials and their joys.

Humour is the keynote of this collection and it opens entertainingly with an extract from Gerald Durrell's *My Family and Other Animals*. More amusement is provided by Helen Cresswell's fantasy of magic in the home, *Particle Goes Green*, and by James Thurber in *The Night the Bed Fell*.

Kipling's haunting story, *The White Seal*, and Jack London's *The Love Master* will appeal to this age-group's feeling for animals, while the neat malice of Saki's *The Lumber Room* and the unexpected twists in Alistair Maclean's *Billy Faa and Hector Macdonald* will make them think.

Myths and legends are well represented by three tales from Greek mythology, the story of Scheherezade from *The Arabian Nights*, and *Finn Mac Coole*, in which Stephen Corrin has skilfully woven stories about the Irish hero into a continuous narrative.

Sara and Stephen Corrin are editors of many popular anthologies for children. Born within the sound of Bow Bells, Sara travels considerably, telling stories, especially in children's libraries, and has made the subject of children's responses to literature one of her main studies. Stephen Corrin was brought up on a mixed diet of the *Gem*, the *Magnet*, the Bible, cricket and Beethoven quartets. He reviews, writes stories, and translates from French, Russian, German and Danish.

Stories for Nine-Year-Olds

and other young readers

EDITED BY

SARA AND STEPHEN CORRIN

Illustrated by Shirley Hughes

Puffin Books

in association with Faber & Faber Ltd

PUFFIN BOOKS

Published by the Penguin Group
Penguin Books Ltd, 27 Wrights Lane, London w8 5tz, England
Viking Penguin, a division of Penguin Books USA Inc.
375 Hudson Street, New York, New York 10014, USA
Penguin Books Australia Ltd, Ringwood, Victoria, Australia
Penguin Books Canada Ltd, 2801 John Street, Markham, Ontario, Canada l3r 1b4
Penguin Books (NZ) Ltd, 182–190 Wairau Road, Auckland 10, New Zealand

Penguin Books Ltd, Registered Offices: Harmondsworth, Middlesex, England

This collection first published by Faber & Faber Ltd 1979
Published in Puffin Books 1981
13 15 17 19 20 18 16 14

Copyright © Faber & Faber Ltd, 1979
Illustrations copyright © Faber & Faber Ltd, 1979
All rights reserved

The acknowledgements on p. 7 constitute an extension of this copyright page.

Printed in England by Clays Ltd, St Ives plc
Set in 12 on 14 pt Monophoto Baskerville

Contents

Contents

Acknowledgements

We are most grateful to the undermentioned publishers, agents and authors for permission to include the following stories:

Rupert Hart-Davis Ltd, Granada Publishing Co. for 'Scorpions in a Matchbox' from *My Family and Other Animals* by Gerald Durrell.

A. M. Heath and Company Ltd for 'Particle Goes Green' by Helen Cresswell, from *Winter's Tales for Children Four*.

The National Trust and Macmillan and Co. of London and Basingstoke for 'The White Seal' from *The Jungle Book* by Rudyard Kipling.

David Higham Associates Ltd for 'Billy Faa and Hector Macdonald' by Alistair Maclean.

'Jean Labadie's Big Black Dog', text only, from *The Talking Cat and Other Stories of French Canada* by Natalie Savage Carlson. Copyright © 1952 by Natalie Savage Carlson. By permission of Harper & Row, Publishers, Inc.

Hamish Hamilton Ltd for 'The Night the Bed Fell' from *Vintage Thurber* by James Thurber. The Collection Copyright © 1963 by Hamish Hamilton Ltd, London.

Jonathan Cape Ltd for 'All You've Ever Wanted' from *All and More* by Joan Aiken.

We should like to thank the Children's Librarians of the London Borough of Barnet; Mary Junor, Schools Librarian, Barnet; the staff of Golders Green Library; and Miss V. Newton, Children's Librarian, Chelsea, for their ever-ready help. We are also most grateful to our colleague Hazel Wilkinson and to Christine Carter, Children's Librarian, Hertfordshire College of Higher Education. Our gratitude to our Editor, Phyllis Hunt, for her painstaking and dedicated care at every step is immeasurable.

To the Reader

We hope that anyone who may have felt that there was a gap between our *Stories for Eight-Year-Olds* and *Stories for Tens and Overs* will welcome this collection. It ranges over many countries and many moods, emphasizing drama and humour but also touching on the sadder and seamier sides of life, while stories from Greek and Celtic mythology strike a note of high adventure.

We feel sure that young readers will be tempted to delve into the other works of the authors represented here.

GERALD DURRELL

Scorpions in a Matchbox

In My Family and Other Animals *Gerald Durrell describes his life with his widowed mother, his brothers and his sister, on the Greek island of Corfu. The numerous animals in the household included scorpions . . .*

The shyest and most self-effacing of the wall community were the most dangerous; you hardly ever saw one unless you looked for it, and yet there must have been several hundred living in the cracks of the wall. Slide a knife-blade carefully under a piece of the loose plaster and lever it gently away from the brick, and there, crouching beneath it, would be a little black scorpion an inch long, looking as though he were made out of polished chocolate. They were weird-looking things, with their flattened, oval bodies, their neat, crooked legs, the enormous crab-like claws, bulbous and neatly jointed as armour, and the tail like a string of brown beads ending in a sting like a rose-thorn. The scorpion would lie there quite quietly as you examined him, only raising his tail in an almost apologetic gesture of warning if you breathed too hard on him. If you kept him in the sun too long he would simply turn his back on you and walk away, and then slide slowly but firmly under another section of plaster.

I grew very fond of these scorpions. I found them to be pleasant, unassuming creatures with, on the whole, the most charming habits. Provided you did nothing silly or clumsy (like putting your hand on one) the scorpions treated you with respect, their one desire being to get away and hide as quickly as possible. They must have found me rather a trial, for I was always ripping sections of the plaster away so that I could watch them, or capturing them and making them walk about in jam-jars so that I could see the way their feet moved. By means of my sudden and unexpected assaults on the wall I discovered quite a bit about the scorpions. I found that they would eat bluebottles (though how they caught them was a mystery I never solved), grasshoppers, moths and lacewing flies. Several times I found them eating each other, a habit I found most distressing in a creature otherwise so impeccable.

By crouching under the wall at night with a torch, I managed to catch some brief glimpses of the scorpions' wonderful courtship dances. I saw them standing, claws clasped, their bodies raised to the skies, their tails lovingly entwined; I saw them waltzing slowly in circles among the moss cushions, claw in claw. But my view of these performances was all too short, for almost as soon as I switched on the torch the partners would stop, pause for a moment, and then, seeing that I was not going to extinguish the light, they would turn round and walk firmly away, claw in claw, side by side. They were definitely beasts that believed in keeping themselves *to* themselves. If I could have kept a colony in captivity I would probably have been able to see the whole of the courtship, but the family had forbidden scorpions in the house, despite my arguments in favour of them.

Then one day I found a fat female scorpion in the wall, wearing what at first glance appeared to be a pale fawn fur coat. Closer inspection proved that this strange garment was made up of a mass of tiny babies clinging to the mother's back. I was enraptured by this family, and I made up my mind to smuggle them into the house and up to my bedroom so that I might keep them and watch them grow up. With infinite care I manoeuvred the mother and family into a matchbox, and then hurried to the villa. It was rather unfortunate that just as I entered the door lunch should be served; however, I placed the matchbox carefully on the mantelpiece in the drawing-room, so that the scorpions should get plenty of air, and made my way to the dining-room and joined the family for the meal. Dawdling over my food, feeding Roger surreptitiously under the table and listening to the family arguing, I completely forgot about my exciting new captures. At last Larry, having finished, fetched the cigarettes from the drawing-room, and lying back in his chair he put one in his mouth and picked up the matchbox he had brought. Oblivious of my impending doom I watched him interestedly as, still talking glibly, he opened the matchbox.

Now I maintain to this day that the female scorpion meant no harm. She was agitated and a trifle annoyed at being shut up in a matchbox for so long, and so she seized the first opportunity to escape. She hoisted herself out of the box with great rapidity, her babies clinging on desperately, and scuttled on to the back of Larry's hand. There, not quite certain what to do next, she paused, her sting curved up at the ready. Larry, feeling the movement of her claws, glanced down to see what it was, and from that moment things got increasingly confused.

He uttered a roar of fright that made Lugaretzia drop a plate and brought Roger out from beneath the table, barking wildly. With a flick of his hand he sent the unfortunate scorpion flying down the table, and she landed midway between Margo and Leslie, scattering babies like confetti as she thumped on the cloth. Thoroughly enraged at this treatment, the creature sped towards Leslie, her sting quivering with emotion. Leslie leapt to his feet, overturning his chair, and flicked out desperately with his napkin, sending the scorpion rolling across the cloth towards Margo, who promptly let out a scream that any railway engine would have been proud to produce. Mother, completely bewildered by this sudden and rapid change from peace to chaos, put on her glasses and peered down the table to see what was causing the pandemonium, and at that moment Margo, in a vain attempt to stop the scorpion's advance, hurled a glass of water at it. The shower missed the animal completely, but successfully drenched Mother, who, not being able to stand cold water, promptly lost her breath and sat gasping at the end of the table, unable even to protest. The scorpion had now gone to ground under Leslie's plate, while her babies swarmed wildly all over the table. Roger, mystified by the panic, but determined to do his share, ran round and round the room, barking hysterically.

'It's that bloody boy again . . .' bellowed Larry.

'Look out! Look out! They're coming!' screamed Margo.

'All we need is a book,' roared Leslie; 'don't panic, hit 'em with a book.'

'What on earth's the *matter* with you all?' Mother kept imploring, mopping her glasses.

'It's that wretched boy . . . he'll kill the lot of us . . . Look at the table . . . knee-deep in scorpions . . .'

'Quick . . . quick . . . do something . . . Look out, look out!'

'Stop screeching and get a book, for God's sake . . . You're worse than the dog . . . Shut *up*, Roger . . .'

'By the Grace of God I wasn't bitten . . .'

'Look out . . . there's another one . . . Quick . . . quick . . .'

15

'Oh, shut up and get me a book or something . . .'

'But *how* did the scorpions get on the table, dear?'

'That bloody boy . . . Every matchbox in the house is a deathtrap . . .'

'Look out, it's coming towards me . . . Quick, quick, do something . . .'

'Hit it with your knife . . . *your* knife . . . Go on, hit it . . .'

Since no one had bothered to explain things to him, Roger was under the mistaken impression that the family were being attacked, and that it was his duty to defend them. As Lugaretzia was the only stranger in the room, he came to the logical conclusion that she must be the responsible party, so he bit her in the ankle. This did not help matters very much.

By the time a certain amount of order had been restored, all the baby scorpions had hidden themselves under various plates and bits of cutlery. Eventually, after impassioned pleas on my part, backed up by Mother, Leslie's suggestion that the whole lot be slaughtered was squashed. While the family, simmering with rage and fright, retired to the drawing-room, I spent half an hour rounding up the babies, picking them up in a teaspoon, and returning them to their mother's back. Then I carried them outside on a saucer and, with the utmost reluctance, released them on the garden wall. Roger and I went and spent the afternoon on the hill-side, for I felt it would be prudent to allow the family to have a siesta before seeing them again . . .

Particle Goes Green

Particle's witchcraft book arrived two days before the Bensons were due to go on holiday. Eve was always the first to the door when the postman came because she was expecting any day to hear that she had won a cabin cruiser in a competition she had entered.

'What's this?' she pondered, examining the parcel. It bore a Sussex postmark. ' "Richard Benson, Esq." – oh, it's that blessed Particle again. Now what?'

She took the book up to her younger brother's bedroom. She had to pick her way over brilliantly splashed sheets of newspaper where he had been action-painting the night before.

'Come on, Particle,' she said. 'Wake up.'

He might, of course, already be awake. It was difficult to see through the mosquito net. He had been sleeping under it for three weeks now, despite the fact that Number 14 Sanders Close rarely saw a bluebottle, let alone a mosquito.

'I am awake,' came his voice. 'Has the post come?'

Eve pulled aside the net. Particle, already wearing his spectacles, was sitting up in bed making clothes-pegs. He had met a gypsy a few days before, camping in a field beyond the town. Particle had presented him with one of Bill's sports jackets, and in return the gypsy had shown him how to make clothes-pegs.

'Really, Particle! Look at all those shavings!'

'I've made fourteen since I woke up,' Particle informed her, in his high, serious voice. 'It's just a question of practice. That, and a bit of knack thrown in. I don't expect I shall ever be quite up to gypsy standard. Peg-making's inborn in them, over generations.'

Eve, despite herself, regarded him fondly.

'He's so refreshing,' she was always telling her friends. 'Honestly, when you think what nine-year-old boys can be like . . . I mean, he's just like a dear little old man, sometimes.'

'Is that for me?' inquired Particle. 'The parcel?'

She handed it over. He gave a couple of expert twists with his jack-knife and the book was in his hands.

'I shan't get up this morning,' he told her. 'I shall stay in bed and read this.'

'What on earth is it? It's not even a new one. It's years old, if you ask me. How much did you pay for it?'

'*Binding Spells*.' He held the book up.

'Binding what?'

'Spells.'

'I've never heard of it. Who by?'

'A witch, I expect,' he said. He turned the flyleaf. 'Look at this – f's instead of s's! It's old, all right!' He was gleeful. 'By Allifon Grofs. The Witch of Northumberland.'

'Oh, Particle. You really are the limit. What on earth possessed you to send for that? And where's it from?'

'An antiquarian bookseller. I wrote to him. I asked him for a book on the subject of witchcraft of the greatest possible antiquity. This is it.'

'How much?' asked Eve. 'We're going on holiday the day after tomorrow, you know. You needn't come borrowing from me if you run out of money half-way through.'

Particle shook the book and a letter fell out. He read it.

'Not all that expensive,' he told her. 'Not considering its antiquity.'

'Well, I should get up, if I were you,' Eve said. 'Bill and Fay aren't going to like this a bit. In fact I expect you've done it on purpose, just to annoy them.'

'Not at all,' said Particle. He really did look like a little old man, propped up against his pillows in his too-large pyjamas and too-large spectacles. 'They should both be very pleased. Witchcraft is an art and a science.'

'I just hope so, that's all,' Eve threw over her shoulder as she went. She paused by her parents' bedroom door. She could hear Bill's voice – they were evidently awake.

'Want a cup of tea?' she called. 'Postman's been.'

'Oh, bless you, darling,' came Fay's voice, and the door opened. Eve kissed her mother and handed her the three letters.

'Nothing for you, dear?'

Eve shook her head.

'Never mind. You know what these competitions are. I'm sure you'll hear soon. That marvellous slogan! I'll be down myself in a minute. I told Bill he could have a lie-in this morning while I scurry round packing, and things.'

Eve nodded and went on down. It was a morning just like any other morning. Even the book on witchcraft didn't mark it as anything special – not at the time. The sunlight fell in pools on the golden oak floor and lit the copper bowl of roses on the chest.

Stepping into the kitchen first thing in the morning was always something of a jolt. It was not really so much a kitchen, Eve thought for the thousandth time, as a laboratory. Apart from that, it came as such a shock after the rest of the house. Whenever people remarked on it, Fay always said:

'Ah, well, of course, the kitchen's Bill's. The rest of the house is pure me, but I gave him a free rein in the kitchen. After all, a kitchen's one place where you must be scientific, mustn't you?'

She would make one of her lovely vague gestures, press a knob and watch a tin opener glide from a concealed socket in the wall, or a waste disposal bin rise from the tiles. The guests would crowd in, enchanted, and Fay would run through the whole performance, igniting cookers, boiling water, making mayonnaise, all by remote control. As her final piece she would always get them to look through the window and then close the front gates under their very eyes. Back in the drawing-room with its oak beams, inglenook and Dresden china, the guests would wonder if they had dreamed it all.

'I'm so thankful I married a scientist,' Fay would coo, drifting in with a tray of sandwiches that had been cut, buttered and filled by Bill's latest recruit to the army of kitchen robots. 'It's so relaxing.'

Eve herself was never so sure. Bill and Fay were both marvellous in their own ways, she appreciated that. It was just that sometimes she felt as if her own personality were being split in two by them, and she herself was a strange hybrid of half-scientist, half-actress. It was so confusing.

Even Particle seemed to suffer from it. The ideas he had, all the outrageous schemes, were straight from Fay. But the precision, the deadly earnestness with which he pursued each one to its logical (or even illogical) conclusion, was unmistakably the same as the passion that drove Bill to pursue electrons into the early hours of the morning, and invent devices so secret that they had to install a concealed safe behind the nineteenth-century print of skaters in the dining-room.

Not that Bill was usually anxious to claim Particle as his own. From the time when Particle had begun to have ideas of his own and put them forward in his high, reedy voice, Bill had been frowning and cross-questioning and finally exploding.

'There isn't a particle of sense in a word you're saying! Not a particle!'

Eve sighed as she regulated the dial for the toast. The holiday began tomorrow – in fact it had as good as started already, since Bill was staying at home – and holidays always seemed to point the problem more sharply. One of these days, she thought, I really shall have to make my mind up. Which am I? Bill or Fay? It occurred to her that even the reason why she and Particle called their parents by their Christian names was not clearcut. Bill believed in it because he thought that 'mummy' and 'daddy' were unscientific, sentimental and probably unhygienic. Fay simply thought that it was modern and rather fun.

When Fay flounced in now, wearing one of her frilled housecoats and the lipstick without which she vowed she couldn't face the milkman, Eve wondered whether it might not be wise to mention the book on witchcraft. She realized that it was bound to produce one of the situations in which the cleft between science and art in the family would yawn into one of its periodic chasms. Fay was already producing from the wall the gadget that was to make her fresh lemon juice. Then the telephone rang and Fay cried:

'Heavens, the phone!' and made a swirling exit.

Eve arranged the neat, popped-up toast, ready curled butter and home (machine) made marmalade on her father's tray. The egg (timed for three minutes twenty seconds precisely) was placed in its stainless-steel heat-retaining egg-cup with its bread (cut to three-eighths of an inch) and ready-spread butter (set at Number 3 – medium heavy spreading).

Satisfied, she picked up the tray, went to the door, trod on the door-operating switch and went into the hall where the newspapers, as if also operated by a timing device, were just appearing through the letter box.

Bill was already up, doing his three minutes' deep breathing by the window. Eve knew better than to interrupt. She laid the tray on the bedside table, blew a kiss towards his intent, reddened face and withdrew.

She went back to Particle's room. He was still in bed.

'Come on,' said Eve. 'Get up. Fay'll never let you stop in bed. There's too much to do.'

From behind the mosquito net came a low, muffled chant. Particle had not even heard her.

'Oh, for heaven's sake!' cried Eve. 'You're not chanting spells, I hope!'

She pulled back the mosquito net. Particle was still propped against his pillows, the book resting on his knees. He broke off, startled. Eve stared at him. She stared so hard that she could feel herself staring, her eyes fixed and bulging. He blinked at her, struck by her expression.

'What's the matter?' he demanded. 'Your eyes are all –'

Then she screamed. She heard herself, too. When the scream, a long, high, frantic one, was out, she ran.

She collided with Fay in the hall.

'Eve! Whatever –?'

Eve faced her mother. For a moment she was speechless. What she had to say was after all, impossible, it must be.

'That scream! And you're white as a ghost. Whatever is it, darling?'

'It's Particle,' Eve heard herself saying. 'He's gone green.' Fay gasped.

'Oh, Eve! Not one of his bilious attacks! Not at a time like this. He can't, he just can't!'

'You don't understand,' cried Eve. 'He's gone green actually!'

'I know it does sometimes seem like it,' agreed Fay.

23

'You'd better take him up some of his usual mixture, and if he stays in bed –'

'Green! Green!' Eve's voice was rising to a scream again.

'I'll go up and have a look,' said Fay. Eve, watching her go up the stairs, had a sudden wild hope that in a moment she would be down again, rummaging round for Particle's tummy mixture and grumbling all the while under her breath, and everything would be miraculously all right again.

Fay's scream was even louder than Eve's. Even Bill heard it – or perhaps by now he had finished his deep breathing anyway. Eve ran up the stairs to find them locked in collision by Particle's door.

'Green!' moaned Fay. 'Oh Bill, I must be going mad!'

'Green?' repeated Bill. 'What's green? Now come along, Fay, pull yourself together. And what's all this screaming?'

'Particle's green!' shrieked Fay. She stepped back and pointed a dramatic finger. 'Look! Go on! Look!'

Bill went into the bedroom. Eve and Fay stared at each other, waiting. Bill came out.

'He is green,' he admitted.

'Pea green!' shrieked Fay. 'Do something, Bill!'

In the silence that followed, Eve was aware of the patter of light footsteps over the bedroom carpet, and for the first time thought of Particle, alone in there, green as grass and probably scared half out of his wits. She pushed past her parents and ran in to find him settling himself against the pillows and pulling up the blankets. His eyes behind the too-large spectacles looked enormous and she fancied that the green was a shade paler now – on his face, at least.

'Oh, Particle,' she said, 'what have you done?'

'I got up,' he said in his high voice, 'and had a look in the mirror . . . I think I had better stay in bed, after all.'

He looked down at his hands, just visible below the cuffs of his tangerine pyjamas. They clashed horribly. Despite herself, Eve could not help noticing with interest that the actual fingernails were still pinkish. Particle, too, was studying them intently, frowning a little.

'Is it – I mean – are you – all over?' asked Eve in a lowered voice.

Without speaking Particle drew a leg from under the bedclothes and waved a skinny, dragonish foot in the air. Eve let out another little scream and Particle looked at her reproachfully.

'I'm sorry, Particle,' she said. 'It's just the shock, you know.'

Particle put his leg back under the blankets. As he did so, the book on witchcraft slid to the floor. Eve seized it.

'It's this!' she cried. 'Isn't it? It's a spell!'

Particle nodded slowly.

'It must be,' he said.

'Which one? Which?' Eve began to thumb feverishly through the pages. She seemed to remember that in all the fairy tales every spell had had an anti-spell, to undo it. That was usually where the good fairy had come in.

'It's no good doing that, you know,' Particle told her. She looked up.

'Why not?'

'This is just Volume 1, Spells and Charms,' he said. 'You need Volume 2 to lift them.'

Eve dropped the book on to the bed. She looked again at Particle with his rumpled hair and calm, perfectly green face and had a sudden wild desire to burst into laughter. Downstairs she could hear the milk bottles being clattered on to the step, and beyond that her parents' high, excited voices. Hearing them reminded her. They did not know about the witchcraft. She made for the door, then turned.

'Wait here,' she ordered. 'Don't move. And don't dare read one other single spell. Don't dare!'

Fay was on the telephone. Eve opened her mouth but Bill held up a warning finger.

'Doctor!' he whispered loudly.

'No . . . no . . .' Fay was saying. 'I mean really green, Doctor. Yes . . . yes . . . he's got plenty of the medicine you gave him last time. No . . . yes . . . but Doctor, I mean actually green. Green!'

Her voice was rising to a shriek again. There was a small pause. 'Yes, yes . . .' her voice trailed off. She put the receiver down.

Eve and Bill looked inquiringly at her.

'He says he'll call tomorrow morning if he's no better,' she said blankly. 'Tomorrow! Oh, Bill! My poor little Particle!'

Bill looked definitely worried.

'Must be some bug or other,' he said. 'Has he got a temperature?'

26

'How do I know if he's got a temperature?' wailed Fay.

'We'll find out,' said Bill. 'Yes, that's the first thing. It should give us a pointer.'

'I've heard of yellow fever,' moaned Fay, 'but this is green! There's no such thing! There's yellow fever and scarlet fever and I'm not sure there isn't a black fever, but I've never in all my life –'

'Now listen,' said Bill, 'you go and make some strong black coffee. There's some perfectly logical explanation for all this, and we'll find it in no time. Some kind of disturbance in pigmentation, perhaps, or faulty diet, or – I'll go and get that thermometer.'

He went out. Eve could see that now he was more interested than worried. He was going to do some research. Just as if poor little Particle were some specimen in a bottle, she thought disgustedly. To Fay she said:

'He needn't bother. There's nothing the matter with Particle – not in that way. It's a spell.'

Fay looked at her. She seemed not to have heard.

'Catching . . .' she murmured. 'What if it's catching?'

'It's witchcraft,' Eve went on. 'Particle sent for a book about it, it came this morning. When I went up just now he was chanting one of the spells. He must have picked the wrong one, or got it mixed up, or something, and –'

She broke off at the expression on Fay's face.

'Witchcraft?' Fay whispered. 'Did you say witch-craft?'

Her face was an alarming, chalky white. It occurred fleetingly to Eve that she didn't seem astonished or even surprised, simply – stunned.

'The Witch of Northumberland, or something,' said Eve. Bill came back with the thermometer.

'Normal,' he said. 'Not even a point in it. The little chap seems to be taking it all quite calmly. "There's bound to be a remedy," he says, cool as a cucumber. Quite scientific about the whole thing. A chip off the old block, after all.'

Eve saw her mother's face change from white to red in an instant.

'Nonsense!' she said sharply.

Bill stared at her.

'All right,' he said, 'no need to be huffy. I merely said that in his whole approach to the thing –'

'I know what you said,' Fay said.

Bill cleared his throat.

'I'll run him down to the surgery,' he said. 'See what Jenkins has to say. No, on second thoughts – the hospital. They've got the equipment there, and so on. This'll be right outside Jenkins's experience.'

'No,' said Fay.

They looked at her.

'Leave him alone,' she said.

'But we're going on holiday the day after tomorrow,' exploded Bill. 'You're not proposing to take a pea-green child to the Royal, I hope. There was enough fuss last year about his marine specimens floating round in the wash basins, and if they once see him –'

'He'll be all right by then,' said Fay.

Bill snorted.

'You mean you hope he'll be all right. If only you could learn the elementary lesson of distinguishing between personal wishes and scientific facts, you'd –'

'He will,' said Fay. She rarely let Bill finish a sentence.

'Fay, can I have my breakfast now?'

It was Particle, in his dressing gown and slippers, looking more than ever like a pantomime hobgoblin, and so obviously impossible among the chintzy chairs and sporting prints that all further discussion was suddenly pointless.

'Of course, darling!' Fay rushed over and hugged him, something she often did, and usually to his annoyance, but this morning he seemed grateful, and even patted a thin green hand on her arm in return.

'Come and have it in the kitchen. Luckily it isn't one of Mrs D's days for coming in, so –' she broke off. 'Oh I'm sorry, darling!'

'It's all right,' said Particle. 'I don't blame you. I do look pretty horrible green.'

'Oh, you don't!' cried Fay, struck with remorse. 'Does he, Eve? You look absolutely sweet, once the first shock of it wears off. Rather like a dear little . . . dear little . . . well, sweet anyway. It's just that Mrs D's such a dreadful gossip, and you can't possibly expect her to understand a thing like this. Now you –'

The door of the kitchen slid across and cut off her voice. Eve looked at Bill. He did not seem anxious to meet her eyes.

29

'Bound to be some scientific explanation,' he said.

'Not this time,' said Eve. It was out at last.

'What do you mean?'

'I mean,' she said, 'that Particle's gone green because there's a spell on him. It's witchcraft.'

Bill stared at her for a moment, then roared with laughter. Eve watched him. Gradually his laughter tailed off rather uneasily under her serious gaze.

'That's rich, that is,' he said.

'Yes, it is,' agreed Eve. 'I thought you'd see the funny side of it.'

'What on earth gave you that idea, anyway?' Bill asked. 'Lord, I've just remembered. My breakfast! I haven't even touched it.'

'It's in your room,' Eve told him. 'And if I were you, I should just take a look at that book on Particle's bed.'

He looked startled, nodded, and went upstairs. Eve settled down to make a list for packing. After a while she became fidgety. Fay and Particle were still in the kitchen. It was not long before she began to wonder if she had imagined the whole thing. Out of sight, a green Particle was even more impossible than when he was actually visible. Eve began to feel that she must have another look, or burst.

She went in. There was no doubt about it. Particle, green as ever, was eating his cornflakes while Fay was fiddling with the toaster. From the way they both looked at her Eve felt certain that they had been in the middle of a very interesting conversation.

'We've decided that the most sensible thing to do is

just to carry on exactly as if nothing had happened,' Fay began.

'Oh?' said Eve. She felt nettled by the indefinable atmosphere of conspiracy that excluded herself. 'Particle's going for his swimming lesson at eleven as usual, is he? That'll be interesting.'

'Almost exactly as if nothing had happened,' Fay amended. 'Obviously Particle's not going parading about outside, but there's nothing to stop the rest of us carrying on as normal. There's plenty for Particle to do about the house. There's all his packing, for a start.'

'Will we be going, then?' Eve asked.

'Yes, we shall,' said Fay firmly.

'But Bill said –'

'Never mind what Bill said. He's far too scientific to have the least inkling of what's happening. And while we're on the subject, Particle and I have decided that it would be best not to mention anything about witchcraft to your father.'

'It's too late,' said Eve. 'I've already told him.'

'What did he say?' gasped Fay.

'He laughed.'

Her mother seemed relieved.

'I'll go up and have a word with him,' she said.

Eve watched her go. All things considered, she seemed to be taking the whole thing very calmly. She turned her attention back to Particle. For someone who was a rich and unbecoming pea green from head to toe and with no immediate prospect of ever being anything else, he too seemed irritatingly unconcerned.

'You know, later on,' he said, 'do you think you could possibly take a colour photo of me? Just for the records?'

'Honestly, Particle,' she cried. 'Fancy thinking of a thing like that at a time like this!'

'If we don't,' said Particle, 'no one's ever going to believe us. In fact about ten years from now we shan't even believe it ourselves.'

Eve shuddered.

'I certainly hope I've forgotten about it long before then,' she told him. Then, rather unkindly, 'If, of course, you're not still green.'

She immediately regretted saying it, but he munched imperturbably and seemed not to have noticed.

'It's all my own fault, of course,' he said.

'Of course it is,' said Eve. 'Who else's?'

'No, I mean for not believing. It said as clear as anything that the spell was for turning people green. I just didn't believe it.'

'I should think not!' cried Eve. 'As if anyone believes in spells and things in this day and age.'

She stopped abruptly. There, set square among the glittering host of electronic gadgets, was the indisputable work of witchcraft. Wherever she looked she could see faint greenish reflections of it in the aluminium and stainless steel. She shivered.

Bill and Fay came in.

'It's all settled,' said Fay almost gaily. 'No hospital and no fuss. Now what does everyone want for lunch?'

It was a queer sort of day all the same. It was not just the frenzied scuffles and panics every time the door bell rang, nor even the sight of Particle himself, more impossible-looking than ever in his faded blue jeans and tee shirt. It was an extraordinary feeling of unreality that intensified as the day went on.

Eve went shopping in the afternoon, and walking down the street felt an almost irresistible urge to greet everyone she met with:

'Have you heard? My brother's gone green! Green as grass from top to toe!'

By the time she reached home her head was aching with the effort of not telling.

Oddly enough the one who was taking it hardest was Bill. At lunchtime Fay and Particle were making silly jokes about his eating up all his greens, and Eve noticed then that Bill was the only one who was not laughing. By teatime he was thoroughly on edge. He sat darting restless, miserable looks at the serenely emerald Particle, and finally burst out:

'Right! That's enough of this whole farce. Get your things on, Particle.'

Particle, half-way through a slice of chocolate cake, blinked inquiringly.

'We're going to the hospital.'

'No,' said Fay.

'If you think I'm going to sit here and watch a son of mine suffering from some obscure and horrible disease without –'

'Nonsense,' said Fay calmly. 'There's not a thing the matter with him.'

'Not a thing the what?' roared Bill. 'Look at him! Just look! We all sit round drinking tea and passing the sugar as if green people grew on trees! I won't have it! I won't have my son that impossible colour. It's impossible! It's beyond all reason!'

They all looked at him.

'It's witchcraft,' said Eve at last.

'Don't keep saying that!' shouted Bill. He lowered his voice. 'I'm sorry. I don't mean to shout. But you must stop all this medieval mumbo-jumbo about witchcraft. We are in the twentieth century. We have electric light. The atom has been split. There is no such thing as witchcraft.'

'I didn't believe it, either,' said Particle.

Bill glared at him, breathing heavily.

'All right!' he said. 'We'll see!'

He stormed out.

'Oh dear,' said Fay. She turned over a cup, the hot tea ran on to Eve's leg, Eve screamed and in the ensuing commotion it was not surprising that no one heard the front door bell ring, or Bill's voice as he spoke to the visitor. They had just settled themselves when the door opened and Bill came in, saying:

'If you'd just like to wait here a moment, Constable, I'll –' His voice tailed away.

There was an enormous, welling, blinding silence. Particle, his chocolate cake poised half-way to his lips, stared at the constable. The constable, his face a mixture of horror and disbelief, stared back. The silence went on and on. It took possession. Isn't anyone going to say anything, thought Eve. Ever?

The policeman gave his head a violent shake, as if to clear his brain or vision. It evidently worked, because he turned his gaze away from Particle and over the others as if looking for clues on their blank faces.

'Good evening, Constable,' said Fay firmly. 'Will you have some tea?' He shook his head.

'No? Perhaps you'd like to sit down a moment while my husband – was it your licence and insurance he wanted to see, dear?'

'I'll get them,' said Bill and vanished.

The constable sat suddenly. Eve looked at him with interest. She had never actually seen a policeman, complete with helmet, sitting in a chair before.

'Won't you take your hat off?' inquired Fay. 'Are

you sure you won't have some tea? Particle, fetch another cup and saucer, will you, darling?'

She's taking it too far, thought Eve. This is one thing she won't talk her way out of.

Particle got up and obediently padded into the kitchen. He was barefoot, as he usually was in the house. The policeman's eyes followed his dragonish feet. Slowly he got to his feet. He cleared his throat.

'That – er – boy . . .' He nodded towards the door.

'Particle?' cried Fay. 'Oh, take no notice of him, Constable. He's always –'

'He's green,' said the constable accusingly.

'Well, yes,' admitted Fay. 'But only temporarily. You see –'

'All over, from what I could see,' he went on. 'From head to foot.'

'Here we are!' It was Bill. 'All in order, I think you'll find.'

The policeman took the documents, examined them with irritating slowness and handed them back.

'Quite in order, sir. Sorry to have troubled you, but it's all part –'

'I know. Quite so. Perhaps I can see you out, if there's nothing else . . .?'

'There's just this other little matter that's arisen, sir.' The constable stood his ground. 'I'd just like to ask one or two questions, sir, if you don't mind. About the green child, sir.'

'Well?' said Bill.

'Well,' said the policeman. 'What about it, sir? I mean, why is the child green?'

'The child is green entirely by his own choice,' said Bill. 'He chooses to be green.'

'Temporarily,' put in Fay.

'I don't like it, sir,' said the policeman flatly. He looked about the room. Eve could tell that he was already beginning to wonder if he was dreaming the whole thing, now that Particle had disappeared.

'As far as I know,' said Bill, 'there's no actual law about people being green. Is there?'

'Well, sir –'

'Or any other colour, as far as I know,' went on Bill. 'As far as I know, a citizen is entitled to adopt any colour he chooses, as long as in so doing he does not constitute a public nuisance. If, for instance, I were to turn bright blue and then go dancing in my bathing trunks on Waterloo Bridge, thereby creating a disturbance and bringing traffic to a halt, that, in my view, would constitute an offence. But as to going green, blue, ginger or buff in the privacy of one's own home, then that's a very different matter indeed, Constable.'

It was at moments like this that Eve could see the advantages of having a scientific mind. The policeman looked distinctly shaken. Then he rallied.

'That's a matter that will have to be gone into, sir,' he said stiffly.

Then Particle returned with the cup and saucer. He grinned, and the flash of white teeth in his green face set the law again into a helpless boggle. Once or twice he opened his mouth as if he were going to say something to Particle, but was uncertain how to go about it, never having addressed a green person before.

'Will you have some tea, Sergeant?' inquired Fay sweetly.

'I shall not stop, thank you, madam,' said the policeman. He rose. 'I'll get along back to the station and make my report.'

'I should think the Inspector will enjoy that,' commented Bill.

'The Inspector will doubtless be calling himself, sir,' said the policeman. 'And the N.S.P.C.C. will have to be informed as well, I'm afraid.'

'The N.S.P. –' Bill stared. Then he and Fay broke into uncontrollable mirth.

'Oh dear!' gasped Fay, her eyes watering.

The constable, with a final outraged glare at their helplessly heaving shoulders, went out. Fay, wiping her eyes, hurried after him, but too late. The front door banged. The laughter stopped abruptly.

'That's done it,' said Bill. 'We shall have Particle's picture plastered over every colour supplement in England now.'

'You don't really think he'll come back, do you?' gurgled Fay. 'Oh, it was so comical. Did you –'

'Comical?' Bill was shouting again. 'Don't you realize what's happened? Don't you care? And what about Particle? Are you mad? Yes, you are!'

'There's no need to shout,' said Fay. 'If you hadn't let him in without warning us first this would never have happened. And now we shall have to do something I didn't want to do at all. Come along, Particle.'

'Oh, Fay,' said Particle. 'I've hardly even got used to the idea yet. Just let me –'

'Come along,' said Fay. He came. Bill and Eve were left staring after them.

'Now what?' muttered Bill. 'I'll go and get the car out.'

'What for?'

'To get Particle away. They'll probably take him away.'

'But why? Particle's just the same as he's always been. He's just green, that's all. I think he's even beginning to enjoy it.'

'So do I,' said Bill grimly. 'I'll get the car.'

Then Fay and Particle came in. Particle was no longer green. The shock was stunning. He looked exactly the same as he always had and yet, for an instant, was a stranger. In that moment Eve felt a curious sense of flatness and disappointment. The vital touch of magic was gone. The room seemed to shrink and settle into itself again. Everything was back to normal. She shivered.

'And what happened?' inquired Bill finally.

'I took the spell away,' said Fay. 'I'm a witch myself, you know. Not a real witch, but descended from witches.'

'Witch?' croaked Bill.

'I know you don't believe in them,' Fay said, 'and if you like we'll forget all about what's happened and not mention it again. I wouldn't have told you if it hadn't been for the policeman. You see all those spells were twenty-four-hour ones – all the Northumberland Witch's are. Particle would have been as right as rain in the morning.'

Particle was over by the mirror examining his face as if looking for any stray patches of green that might have been left. When he turned away Eve could see that he, too, was disappointed.

'We never even took those colour photos,' he said.

'You could try again, some time,' said Eve.

'It's no good. Fay said that was a chance in a million. You're supposed to be a seventh child of a seventh child, and I'm only the second. Fay says that the law of heredity –'

'Ah!' Bill's face brightened. 'Heredity. Now as I see it, what happened was this, Fay herself, being the seventh child of a –'

'Sixth,' said Fay.

'Pardon?'

'Sixth child of a seventh child,' said Fay. 'I told you, I'm not a real witch, any more than Particle is. We just have our moments.'

She and Particle exchanged smug glances. Bill said, 'I'm going to make some more tea.'

They all followed him into the kitchen.

'Aaah!' Bill let out a long breath and looked around him with relief. He was on home territory. He fiddled with his dials for a long time, grateful for something that he could understand.

'You know,' he said then, 'it's obvious now what happened today.'

'Oh?' said Fay.

'Yes. Mass hysteria. It's a well known phenomenon. You see, Eve, knowing that Particle had a book on witchcraft, subconsciously –'

The front door bell rang.

'I think that this,' said Fay, 'will be the police. And the N.S.P.C.C. And the reporters.'

Then Bill said, 'I think Particle had better answer the door, don't you?'

The Bensons looked at each other with sudden glee. Eve thought fleetingly, 'Particle said witchcraft was an art and a science', and then they were all crowding into the hall to see the fun. Because tomorrow it was going to be difficult to believe that any of this had happened at all, and the day after, harder still . . .

STEPHEN CORRIN

Scheherezade

There was once a King of Persia named Shahryar who was most devoted to his beautiful Queen. He thought she was a most faithful and loyal wife to him. She, however, only *pretended* to be devoted to *him*. One day Shahryar's brother, who used to go hunting with him, felt ill and stayed behind in the palace while the King was away. Through the window of his room he was horrified to see the Queen unveil her face in the presence of the courtiers. Now you must understand that in the Persia of those days a woman was strictly forbidden to do this and, besides, the King had expressly instructed her not to leave her rooms.

When the King returned from the hunt, his brother told him what he had seen but the King became angry and refused to believe him. He took his brother's advice, however, and the following day he himself secretly stayed behind in the palace though he gave out officially that he had gone hunting. To his indescribable shock and grief he beheld through the window what his brother had seen the previous afternoon. His anger knew no bounds when he realized that he had been deceived by the wife whom he had always trusted. He ordered her to be executed immediately, while he himself shut himself up in a room and refused to eat or drink for several days. At last his brother persuaded him to come out and resume his royal duties. But his fury over what had happened remained as great as ever and he made a fearsome vow, in the name of Allah, that whatever new queen he might marry should be executed the morning after the wedding. By doing this he thought he would calm his anger and at the same time avenge himself on all wives for what his own wife had done to him. He decided to keep on re-marrying and have every one of his queens executed after the marriage.

And that is what happened; and it went on for many months and every person who had a daughter of marriageable age tried to find ways and means of sending her away to a safe hiding place.

Now King Shahryar's prime minister, the Grand Vizier as he was called, had two beautiful daughters of his own, Scheherezade and Dinarzade. Scheherezade was a most unusual girl, extremely learned, incredibly beautiful and full of good common sense. She knew that one day, sooner or later, she would be compelled to become the King's wife, but in her wise and lovely head she thought of a plan that would save not only herself but all the other Persian girls whose lot it might be to become Shahryar's wife.

One day the Grand Vizier returned from the palace and told his daughters the dread news that the King had decided that Scheherezade was to be his next Queen. But Scheherezade was quite prepared for this and said, 'Honoured father, let us do as the King wishes. Have trust in me and one day you will see an end to this monstrous cruelty.' Her father was speechless with horror. 'How can you say that, dear daughter,' he exclaimed, 'when you know full well that the day after your marriage you will be put to death by the King's very command? No, my daughter, this can never be! Your life is too precious to be disposed of in this terrible way. Tonight you and your sister will steal out of the city to a place of safety. If a life *must* be sacrificed, then let it be mine! I shall face the King and tell him that I will not allow *my* daughters to be treated thus.' But when he started giving orders for the whole household to prepare for a secret flight into hiding, Scheherezade told him firmly, 'Dear father, if you will not take me to the palace I shall go there myself and offer myself as wife to King Shahryar.' And she again tried to assure her almost demented father that everything would turn out well if he would only trust her.

When the Grand Vizier saw how firm his daughter was in her resolve, he gave way. Scheherezade put on her bridal garments, ornamented her hair with pearls and her arms with bracelets, covered her face with a veil of the costliest silk and sprayed herself with seductive perfumes. She looked so enchanting that her attendants wept to think that so magnificent a creature was walking straight to her death.

Then Scheherezade took her sister, Dinarzade, into a room by themselves and said to her, 'You, dear sister, must play an important part in the plan I have devised to save myself and you and all the young women of Persia.' Dinarzade looked at her in great astonishment. Scheherezade continued, 'You know how much you have enjoyed the stories I have so often told you. Well, before I am to be put to death, I shall ask the King as a special favour, to allow you to come and listen to just one more story in his presence. So when I send for you, you must come to the palace.'

'Yes, dear sister,' replied Dinarzade, her eyes filled with tears, 'of course I shall come.'

Scheherezade was duly conducted to the palace by her father and her personal attendants. The King was greatly impressed by her beauty and the marriage was celebrated amid great pomp and ceremony.

After the wedding the new Queen said to her husband, 'When a prisoner is condemned to death, he is allowed one last request. As I am to die tomorrow morning, may I, as my final wish on this earth, say goodbye to my sister?' Her request was granted and Dinarzade was soon at her sister's side in the palace. She wept bitterly as she said her farewell and Scheherezade could see that even the King looked somewhat sorrowful at the scene. She cleverly took advantage of this softening in his mood and asked him whether she might be allowed to tell her sister a favourite story that she had often told her in the past. King Shahryar, it so happened, was also very fond of listening to stories and so he willingly consented.

And now Scheherezade, in her lovely low voice, began to tell a most interesting story. King Shahryar listened, quite relaxed at first, but more attentively as the story got more and more exciting. But when she got to the most breathlessly exciting part she paused and said to her sister, 'I fear, dear Dinarzade, that you must leave now, for His Majesty is tired and wishes to retire to his bed.'

'No, please continue,' said the King.

'There is much more to come,' replied Scheherezade. 'I could continue tomorrow if my life were spared for one more day.'

'Very well,' said the King a trifle impatiently, and so Dinarzade went home but promised to come back the next day. The King thought to himself, 'There is no need to have her executed tomorrow, I can always wait another day, but I must hear the end of that story whatever happens.' But he was reckoning without Scheherezade's amazing gift for telling stories and, what was more important, her knack of breaking off just at the most exciting or puzzling point of the story. The Grand Vizier, you may well imagine, was astonished when he discovered that his daughter's execution had been postponed.

So the next day Dinarzade arrived at the palace and King Shahryar ordered Scheherezade to continue her story and she did, with a vengeance! She went on and on, increasing the excitement and the thrills so that when it finally came to an end the King asked her to tell another story! He was thinking to himself, 'First let me hear her tell another exciting tale, there is no great hurry for her execution.'

Now Scheherezade knew more than a thousand stories and she told them to the King night after night but always breaking off at the most intriguing part and leaving her listener in such a state of suspense that he kept asking for more.

After a thousand and one nights had passed in this way, Scheherezade, instead of starting a new story, turned to the King and said, 'It seems, Your Majesty, that you have not been displeased with my stories. If I have found favour in Your Majesty's eyes, may I now ask for some reward?' The King felt somewhat ashamed, for it was the custom of Persian monarchs always to reward even their humblest subjects for any small service, and yet he had given nothing, nothing at all to his own Queen!

Scheherezade took advantage of his silence to continue. 'You once made a most dreadful vow,' she said, 'but Allah would certainly not ask from you that you should fulfil so evil a pledge.'

The King had listened attentively, just as he had listened to her stories and he felt a deep guilt in his heart.

'My Queen,' he began, 'I now know that I have been too hasty and that I should never have made that evil vow. Why indeed should you suffer because of the wrongdoing of my first wife? Besides, I have myself already wronged too many innocent girls in my kingdom and I must make handsome amends to their families.' And he immediately caused it to be proclaimed from his palace that he had forsaken his terrible vow and praised his Queen Scheherezade as the most excellent of women and the most devoted of wives.

The people were relieved and overjoyed at this tremendous change in the King's mood and in gratitude to their wonderful Queen they renamed their capital city after her, for the name Scheherezade itself means Saviour of the City: the name given to her at birth proved truly prophetic! And the tales she told have come down to us as *The Arabian Nights* or, sometimes, *The Thousand and One Nights*.

RUDYARD KIPLING

The White Seal

Oh! hush thee, my baby, the night is behind us,
  And black are the waters that sparkled so green.
The moon, o'er the combers, looks downward to find us
  At rest in the hollows that rustle between.
Where billow meets billow, there soft be thy pillow;
  Ah, weary wee flipperling, curl at thy ease!
The storm shall not wake thee, nor shark overtake thee,
  Asleep in the arms of the slow-swinging seas.

Seal Lullaby

All these things happened several years ago at a place called Novastoshnah, or North-East Point, on the Island of St Paul, away and away in the Bering Sea. Limmershin, the Winter Wren, told me the tale when he was blown on to the rigging of a steamer going to Japan, and I took him down into my cabin and warmed and fed him for a couple of days till he was fit to fly back to St Paul's again. Limmershin is a very odd little bird, but he knows how to tell the truth.

Nobody comes to Novastoshnah except on business, and the only people who have regular business there are the seals. They come in the summer months by hundreds and hundreds of thousands out of the cold grey sea; for Novastoshnah Beach has the finest accommodation for seals of any place in all the world.

Sea Catch knew that, and every spring would swim from whatever place he happened to be in – would swim like a torpedo-boat straight for Novastoshnah, and spend a month fighting with his companions for a good place on the rocks as close to the sea as possible. Sea Catch was fifteen years old, a huge grey fur-seal with almost a mane on his shoulders, and long, wicked dog-teeth. When he heaved himself up on his front flippers he stood more than four feet clear of the ground, and his weight, if anyone had been bold enough to weigh him, was nearly seven hundred pounds. He was scarred all over with the marks of savage figghts, but he was always ready for just one fight more. He would put his head on one side, as though he were afraid to look his enemy in the face; then he would shoot it out like lightning, and when the big teeth were firmly fixed on the other seal's neck, the other seal might get away if he could, but Sea Catch would not help him.

Yet Sea Catch never chased a beaten seal, for that was against the Rules of the Beach. He only wanted room by the sea for his nursery; but as there were forty or fifty thousand other seals hunting for the same thing each spring, the whistling, bellowing, roaring, and blowing on the beach were something frightful.

From a little hill called Hutchinson's Hill you could look over three and a half miles of ground coovered with fighting seals; and the surf was dotted all over with the heads of seals hurrying to land and begin their share of the fighting. They fought in the breakers, they fought in the sand, and they fought on the smooth-worn basalt rocks of the nurseries; for they were just as stupid and unaccommodating as men. Their wives never came to the island until late in May or early in June, for they did not care to be torn to pieces; and the young two-, three-, and four-year-old seals who had not begun housekeeping went inland about half a mile through the ranks of the fighters and played about on the sand-dunes in droves and legions, and rubbed off every single green thing that grew. They were called the holluschickie – the bachelors – and there were perhaps two or three hundred thousand of them at Novastoshnah alone.

Sea Catch had just finished his forty-fifth fight one spring when Matkah, his soft, sleek, gentle-eyed wife, came up out of the sea, and he caught her by the scruff of the neck and dumped her down on his reservation, saying gruffly: 'Late, as usual. Where *have* you been?'

It was not the fashion for Sea Catch to eat anything during the four months he stayed on the beaches, and so his temper was generally bad. Matkah knew better than to answer back. She looked round and cooed: 'How thoughtful of you! You've taken the old place again.'

'I should think I had,' said Sea Catch. 'Look at me!'

He was scratched and bleeding in twenty places; one eye was almost blind, and his sides were torn to ribbons.

'Oh, you men, you men!' Matkah said, fanning herself with her hind flipper. 'Why can't you be sensible and settle your places quietly? You look as though you had been fighting with the Killer Whale.'

'I haven't been doing anything *but* fight since the

51

middle of May. The beach is disgracefully crowded this season. I've met at least a hundred seals from Lukannon Beach, house-hunting. Why can't people stay where they belong?'

'I've often thought we should be much happier if we hauled out at Otter Island instead of this crowded place,' said Matkah.

'Bah! Only the holluschickie go to Otter Island. If we went there they would say we were afraid. We must preserve appearances, my dear.'

Sea Catch sunk his head proudly between his fat shoulders and pretended to go to sleep for a few minutes, but all the time he was keeping a sharp lookout for a fight. Now that all the seals and their wives were on the land, you could hear their clamour miles out to sea above the loudest gales. At the lowest counting there were over a million seals on the beach – old seals, mother seals, tiny babies, and holluschickie, fighting, scuffling, bleating, crawling and playing together – going down to the sea and coming up from it in gangs and regiments, lying over every foot of ground as far as the eye could reach, and skirmishing about in brigades through the fog. It is nearly always foggy at Novastoshnah, except when the sun comes out and makes everything look all pearly and rainbow-coloured for a little while.

Kotick, Matkah's baby, was born in the middle of that confusion, and he was all head and shoulders, with pale, watery-blue eyes, as tiny seals must be; but there was something about his coat that made his mother look at him very closely.

'Sea Catch,' she said at last, 'our baby's going to be white!'

'Empty clam-shells and dry seaweed!' snorted Sea Catch. 'There never has been such a thing in the world as a white seal.'

'I can't help that,' said Matkah; 'there's going to be now;' and she sang the low, crooning seal-song that all the mother seals sing to their babies:

> *You mustn't swim till you're six weeks old,*
> *Or your head will be sunk by your heels;*
> *And summer gales and Killer Whales*
> *Are bad for baby seals.*

> *Are bad for baby seals, dear rat,*
> *As bad as bad can be;*
> *But splash and grow strong,*
> *And you can't be wrong,*
> *Child of the Open Sea!*

Of course the little fellow did not understand the words at first. He paddled and scrambled about his mother's side, and learned to scuffle out of the way when his father was fighting with another seal, and the two rolled and roared up and down the slippery rocks. Matkah used to go to sea to get things to eat, and the baby was fed only once in two days; but then he ate all he could, and throve upon it.

The first thing he did was to crawl inland, and there he met tens of thousands of babies of his age, and they played together like puppies, went to sleep on the clean sand, and played again. The old people in the nurseries took no notice of them, and the holluschickie kept to their own grounds, so the babies had a beautiful play-time.

When Matkah came back from her deep-sea fishing she would go straight to their playground and call as a sheep calls for a lamb, and wait until she heard Kotick bleat. Then she would take the straightest of straight lines in his direction, striking out with her fore flippers and knocking the youngsters head over heels right and left. There were always a few hundred mothers hunting for their children through the playgrounds, and the babies were kept lively; but, as Matkah told Kotick, 'So long as you don't lie in muddy water and get mange, or rub the hard sand into a cut or scratch, and so long as you never go swimming when there is a heavy sea, nothing will hurt you here.'

Little seals can no more swim than little children, but they are unhappy till they learn. The first time that Kotick went down to the sea a wave carried him out beyond his depth, and his big head sank and his little hind flippers flew up exactly as his mother had told him in the song, and if the next wave had not thrown him back again he would have drowned.

After that he learned to lie in a beach-pool and let the wash of the waves just cover him and lift him up while he paddled, but he always kept his eye open for big waves that might hurt. He was two weeks learning to use his flippers; and all that while he floundered in and out of the water, and coughed and grunted and crawled up the beach and took cat naps on the sand,

and went back again, until at last he found that he truly belonged to the water.

Then you can imagine the times that he had with his companions, ducking under the rollers; or coming in on top of a comber and landing with a swash and a splutter as the big wave went whirling far up the beach; or standing up on his tail and scratching his head as the old people did; or playing 'I'm the King of the Castle' on slippery, weedy rocks that just stuck out of the wash. Now and then he would see a thin fin, like a big shark's fin, drifting along close to shore, and he knew that that was the Killer Whale, the Grampus, who eats young seals when he can get them; and Kotick would head for the beach like an arrow, and the fin would jig off slowly, as if it were looking for nothing at all.

Late in October the seals began to leave St Paul's for the deep sea, by families and tribes, and there was no more fighting over the nurseries, and the holluschickie played anywhere they liked. 'Next year,' said Matkah to Kotick, 'you will be a holluschickie; but this year you must learn how to catch fish.'

They set out together across the Pacific, and Matkah showed Kotick how to sleep on his back with his flippers tucked down by his side and his little nose just out of the water. No cradle is so comfortable as the long, rocking swell of the Pacific. When Kotick felt his skin tingle all over, Matkah told him he was learning the 'feel of the water', and that tingly, prickly feelings meant bad weather coming, and he must swim hard and get away.

'In a little time,' she said, 'you'll know where to

swim to, but just now we'll follow Sea Pig, the Por-poise, for he is very wise.' A school of porpoises were ducking and tearing through the water, and little Kotick followed them as fast as he could. 'How do you know where to go to?' he panted. The leader of the school rolled his white eyes, and ducked under. 'My tail tingles, youngster,' he said. 'That means there's a gale behind me. Come along! When you're south of the Sticky Water [he meant the Equator], and your tail tingles, that means there's a gale in front of you and you must head north. Come along! The water feels bad here.'

This was one of the very many things that Kotick learned, and he was always learning. Matkah taught him to follow the cod and the halibut along the under-sea banks, and wrench the rockling out of his hole among the weeds; how to skirt the wrecks lying a hun-dred fathoms below water, and dart like a rifle-bullet in at one porthole and out at another as the fishes ran; how to dance on the top of the waves when the light-ning was racing all over the sky, and wave his flipper politely to the stumpy-tailed Albatross and the Man-of-war Hawk as they went down the wind; how to jump three or four feet clear of the water, like a dol-phin, flippers close to the side and tail curved; to leave the flying fish alone because they are all bony; to take the shoulder-piece out of a cod at full speed ten fath-oms deep; and never to stop and look at a boat or a ship, but particularly a row-boat. At the end of six months, what Kotick did not know about deep-sea fish-ing was not worth knowing, and all that time he never set flipper on dry ground.

One day, however, as he was lying half asleep in the warm water somewhere off the Island of Juan Fernandez, he felt faint and lazy all over, just as human people do when the spring is in their legs, and he remembered the good firm beaches of Novastoshnah seven thousand miles away, the games his companions played, the smell of the seaweed, the seal roar and the fighting. That very minute he turned north, swimming steadily, and as he went on he met scores of his mates, all bound for the same place, and they said: 'Greeting, Kotick! This year we are all holluschickie, and we can dance the Fire-dance in the breakers off Lukannon and play on the new grass. But where did you get that coat?'

Kotick's fur was almost pure white now, and though he felt very proud of it, he only said: 'Swim quickly! My bones are aching for the land.' And so they all came to the beaches where they had been born, and heard the old seals, their fathers, fighting in the rolling mist.

That night Kotick danced the Fire-dance with the yearling seals. The sea is full of fire on summer nights all the way down from Novastoshnah to Lukannon, and each seal leaves a wake like burning oil behind him, and a flaming flash when he jumps, and the waves break in great phosphorescent streaks and swirls. Then they went inland to the holluschickie grounds, and rolled up and down in the new wild wheat, and told stories of what they had done while they had been at sea. They talked about the Pacific as boys would talk about a wood that they had been nutting in, and if anyone had understood them, he could have gone away and made such a chart of that ocean as never was. The three- and four-year-old holluschickie romped down from Hutchinson's Hill, crying: 'Out of the way, youngsters! The sea is deep, and you don't know all that's in it yet. Wait till you've rounded the Horn. Hi, you yearling, where did you get that white coat?'

'I didn't get it,' said Kotick; 'it grew.' And just as he was going to roll the speaker over, a couple of black-haired men with flat red faces came from behind a sand-dune, and Kotick, who had never seen a man before, coughed and lowered his head. The holluschickie just bundled off a few yards and sat staring stupidly. The men were no less than Kerick Booterin, the chief of the seal-hunters on the island, and Patalamon, his son. They came from the little village not half a mile from the seal-nurseries, and they were deciding what seals they would drive up to the killing-pens (for the seals were driven just like sheep), to be turned into sealskin jackets later on.

'Ho!' said Patalamon. 'Look! There's a white seal!'

Kerick Booterin turned nearly white under his oil and smoke, for he was an Aleut, and Aleuts are not clean people. Then he began to mutter a prayer. 'Don't touch him, Patalamon. There has never been a white seal since – since I was born. Perhaps it is old Zaharrof's ghost. He was lost last year in the big gale.'

'I'm not going near him,' said Patalamon. 'He's unlucky. Do you really think he is old Zaharrof come back? I owe him for some gulls' eggs.'

'Don't look at him,' said Kerick. 'Head off that

drove of four-year-olds. The men ought to skin two hundred today, but it's the beginning of the season, and they are new to the work. A hundred will do. Quick!'

Patalamon rattled a pair of seal's shoulder-bones in front of a herd of holluschickie, and they stopped dead, puffing and blowing. Then he stepped near, and the seals began to move, and Kerick headed them inland, and they never tried to get back to their companions. Hundreds and hundreds of thousands of seals watched them being driven, but they went on playing just the same. Kotick was the only one who asked questions, and none of his companions could tell him anything, except that the men always drove seals in that way for six weeks or two months of every year.

'I am going to follow,' he said, and his eyes nearly popped out of his head as he shuffled along in the wake of the herd.

'The white seal is coming after us,' cried Patalamon. 'That's the first time a seal has ever come to the killing-grounds alone.'

'Hsh! Don't look behind you,' said Kerick. 'It *is* Zaharrof's ghost! I must speak to the priest about this.'

The distance to the killing-grounds was only half a mile, but it took an hour to cover, because if the seals went too fast Kerick knew that they would get heated and then their fur would come off in patches when they were skinned. So they went on very slowly, past Sea-Lion's Neck, past Webster House, till they came to the Salt House just beyond the sight of the seals on the beach. Kotick followed, panting and wondering. He thought that he was at the world's end, but the roar of the seal-nurseries behind him sounded as loud as the roar of a train in a tunnel. Then Kerick sat down on the moss and pulled out a heavy pewter watch and let the drove cool off for thirty minutes, and Kotick could hear the fog-dew dripping from the brim of his cap. Then ten or twelve men, each with an iron-bound club three or four feet long, came up, and Kerick pointed out one or two of the drove that were bitten by their companions or were too hot, and the men kicked those aside with their heavy boots made of the skin of a walrus's throat, and then Kerick said: 'Let go!' and then the men clubbed the seals on the head as fast as they could.

Ten minutes later Kotick did not recognize his

friends any more, for their skins were ripped off from
the nose to the hind flippers – whipped off and thrown
down on the ground in a pile.

That was enough for Kotick. He turned and galloped (a seal can gallop very swiftly for a short time)
back to the sea, his little new moustache bristling with
horror. At Sea-Lion's Neck, where the great sea-lions
sit on the edge of the surf, he flung himself flipper over
head into the cool water, and rocked there, gasping
miserably. 'What's here?' said a sea-lion gruffly; for as
a rule the sea-lions keep themselves to themselves.

'*Scoochnie! Ochen scoochnie!* [I'm lonesome, very lonesome!]' said Kotick. 'They're killing all the holluschickie on *all* the beaches!'

The sea-lion turned his head inshore. 'Nonsense!' he
said; 'your friends are making as much noise as ever.
You must have seen old Kerick polishing off a drove.
He's done that for thirty years.'

'It's horrible,' said Kotick, backing water as a wave
went over him, and steadying himself with a screw-
stroke of his flippers that brought him up all standing
within three inches of a jagged edge of rock.

'Well done for a yearling!' said the sea-lion, who
could appreciate good swimming. 'I suppose it *is* rather
awful from your way of looking at it; but if you seals
will come here year after year, of course the men get to
know of it, and unless you can find an island where no
men ever come, you will always be driven.'

'Isn't there any such island?' began Kotick.

'I've followed the *poltoos* [the halibut] for twenty
years, and I can't say I've found it yet. But look here –

you seem to have a fondness for talking to your betters; suppose you go to Walrus Islet and talk to Sea Vitch. He may know something. Don't flounce off like that. It's a six-mile swim, and if I were you I should haul out and take a nap first, little one.'

Kotick thought that that was good advice, so he swam round to his own beach, hauled out, and slept for half an hour, twitching all over, as seals will. Then he headed straight for Walrus Islet, a little low sheet of rocky island almost due north-east from Novastoshnah, all ledges of rocks and gulls' nests, where the walrus herded by themselves.

He landed close to old Sea Vitch – the big, ugly, bloated, pimpled, fat-necked, long-tusked walrus of the North Pacific, who has no manners except when he is asleep – as he was then, with his hind flippers half in and half out of the surf.

'Wake up!' barked Kotick, for the gulls were making a great noise.

'Ha! Ho! Hmph! What's that?' said Sea Vitch, and he struck the next walrus a blow with his tusks and waked him up, and the next struck the next, and so on till they were all awake and staring in every direction but the right one.

'Hi! It's me,' said Kotick, bobbing in the surf and looking like a little white slug.

'Well! May I be – skinned!' said Sea Vitch, and they all looked at Kotick as you can fancy a club full of drowsy old gentlemen would look at a little boy. Kotick did not care to hear any more about skinning just then; he had seen enough of it; so he called out:

'Isn't there any place for seals to go where men don't ever come?'

'Go and find out,' said Sea Vitch, shutting his eyes. 'Run away. We're busy here.'

Kotick made his dolphin-jump in the air and shouted as loud as he could: 'Clam-eater! Clam-eater!' He knew that Sea Vitch never caught a fish in his life, but always rooted for clams and seaweeds, though he pretended to be a very terrible person. Naturally the Chickies and the Gooverooskies and the Epatkas, the Burgomaster Gulls and the Kittiwakes and the Puffins, who are always looking for a chance to be rude, took up the cry, and – so Limmershin told me – for nearly five minutes you could not have heard a gun fired on Walrus Islet. All the population was yelling and screaming; 'Clam-eater! *Stareek* [old man!]' while Sea Vitch rolled from side to side grunting and coughing.

'*Now* will you tell?' said Kotick, all out of breath.

'Go and ask Sea Cow,' said Sea Vitch. 'If he is living still, he'll be able to tell you.'

'How shall I know Sea Cow when I meet him?' said Kotick, sheering off.

'He's the only thing in the sea uglier than Sea Vitch,' screamed a Burgomaster Gull, wheeling under Sea Vitch's nose. 'Uglier, and with worse manners! *Stareek!*'

Kotick swam back to Novastoshnah, leaving the gulls to scream. There he found that no one sympathized with him in his little attempts to discover a quiet place for the seals. They told him that men had always driven the holluschickie – it was part of the day's work

63

– and that if he did not like to see ugly things he should not have gone to the killing-grounds. But none of the other seals had seen the killing, and that made the difference between him and his friends. Besides, Kotick was a white seal.

'What you must do,' said old Sea Catch, after he had heard his son's adventures, 'is to grow up and be a big seal like your father, and have a nursery on the beach, and then they will leave you alone. In another five years you ought to be able to fight for yourself.' Even gentle Matkah, his mother, said: 'You will never be able to stop the killing. Go and play in the sea, Kotick.' And Kotick went off and danced the Fire-dance with a very heavy little heart.

That autumn he left the beach as soon as he could, and set off alone because of a notion in his bullet-head. He was going to find Sea Cow, if there was such a person in the sea, and he was going to find a quiet island with good firm beaches for seals to live on, where men could not get at them. So he explored and explored by himself from the North to the South Pacific, swimming as much as three hundred miles in a day and a night. He met with more adventures than can be told, and narrowly escaped being caught by the Basking Shark and the Spotted Shark, and the Hammerhead, and he met all the untrustworthy ruffians that loaf up and down the seas, and the heavy polite fish, and the scarlet-spotted scallops that are moored in one place for hundreds of years, and grow very proud of it; but he never met Sea Cow, and he never found an island that he could fancy.

If the beach was good and hard, with a slope behind it for seals to play on, there was always the smoke of a whaler on the horizon, boiling down blubber, and Kotick knew what *that* meant. Or else he could see that seals had once visited the island and been killed off, and Kotick knew that where men had come once they would come again.

He picked up with an old stumpy-tailed albatross, who told him that Kerguelen Island was the very place for peace and quiet, and when Kotick went down there he was all but smashed to pieces against some wicked black cliffs in a heavy sleet-storm with lightning and thunder. Yet as he pulled out against the gale he could see that even there had once been a seal-nursery. And so it was in all the other islands that he visited.

Limmershin gave a long list of them, for he said that Kotick spent five seasons exploring, with a four months' rest each year at Novastoshnah, when the holluschickie used to make fun of him and his imaginary islands. He went to the Galapagos, a horrid dry place on the Equator, where he was nearly baked to death; he went to the Georgia Island, the South Orkneys, Emerald Island, Little Nightingale Island, Gough's Island, Bouvet's Island, the Crossets, and even to a little speck of an island south of the Cape of Good Hope. But everywhere the People of the Sea told him the same things. Seals had come to those islands once upon a time, but men had killed them all off. Even when he swam thousands of miles out of the Pacific, and got to a place called Cape Corrientes (that was when he was coming back from Gough's Island), he

65

found a few hundred mangy seals on a rock, and they told him that men came there too.

That nearly broke his heart, and he headed round the Horn back to his own beaches; and on his way north he hauled out on an island full of green trees, where he found an old, old seal who was dying, and Kotick caught fish for him, and told him all his sorrows. 'Now,' said Kotick, 'I am going back to Novastoshnah, and if I am driven to the killing-pens with the holluschickie I shall not care.'

The old seal said: 'Try once more. I am the last of the Lost Rookery of Masafuera, and in the days when men killed us by the hundred thousand there was a story on the beaches that some day a white seal would come out of the north and lead the seal people to a quiet place. I am old and I shall never live to see that day, but others will. Try once more.'

And Kotick curled up his moustache (it was a beauty), and said: 'I am the only white seal that has ever been born on the beaches, and I am the only seal, black or white, who ever thought of looking for new islands.'

That cheered him immensely; and when he came-back to Novastoshnah that summer, Matkah, his mother, begged him to marry and settle down, for he was no longer a holluschick, but a full-grown sea-catch, with a curly white mane on his shoulders, as heavy, as big and as fierce as his father. 'Give me another season,' he said. 'Remember, mother, it is always the seventh wave that goes farthest up the beach.'

Curiously enough, there was another seal who

thought that she would put off marrying till the next year, and Kotick danced the Fire-dance with her all down Lukannon Beach the night before he set off on his last exploration.

This time he went westward, because he had fallen on the trail of a great shoal of halibut, and he needed at least one hundred pounds of fish a day to keep him in good condition. He chased them till he was tired, and then he curled himself up and went to sleep on the hollows of the ground-swell that sets in to Copper Island. He knew the coast perfectly well, so about midnight, when he felt himself gently bumped on a weed-bed, he said, 'Hm, tide's running strong tonight,' and turning over under water opened his eyes slowly and stretched. Then he jumped like a cat, for he saw huge things nosing about in the shoal water and browsing on the heavy fringes of the weeds.

'By the Great Combers of Magellan!' he said, beneath his moustache. 'Who in the Deep Sea are these people?'

They were like no walrus, sea-lion, seal bear, whale, shark, fish, squid or scallop that Kotick had ever seen before. They were between twenty and thirty feet long, and they had no hind flippers, but a shovel-like tail that looked as if it had been whittled out of wet leather. Their heads were the most foolish-looking things you ever saw, and they balanced on the ends of their tails in deep water when they weren't grazing, bowing solemnly to one another and waving their front flippers as a fat man waves his arm.

'Ahem!' said Kotick. 'Good sport, gentlemen?' The

big things answered by bowing and waving their flippers like the Frog-Footman. When they began feeding again Kotick saw that their upper lip was split into two pieces that they could twitch apart about a foot and bring together again with a whole bushel of seaweed between the splits. They tucked the stuff into their mouths and chumped solemnly.

'Messy style of feeding, that,' said Kotick. They bowed again, and Kotick began to lose his temper.

'Very good,' he said. 'If you do happen to have an extra joint in your front flipper you needn't show off so. I see you bow gracefully, but I should like to know your names.' The split lips moved and twitched, and the glassy green eyes stared; but they did not speak.

'Well!' said Kotick. 'You're the only people I've ever met uglier than Sea-Vitch – and with worse manners.'

Then he remembered in a flash what the Burgomaster Gull had screamed to him when he was a little yearling at Walrus Islet, and he tumbled backwards in the water, for he knew that he had found Sea Cow at last.

The sea cows went on schlooping and grazing and chumping in the weed, and Kotick asked them questions in every language that he had picked up in his travels: and the Sea People talk nearly as many languages as human beings. But the Sea Cow did not answer, because Sea Cow cannot talk. He has only six bones in his neck where he ought to have seven, and they say under the sea that that prevents him from speaking even to his companions; but, as you know, he has an extra joint in his fore flipper, and by waving it up and down and about he makes a sort of clumsy telegraphic code.

By daylight Kotick's mane was standing on end and his temper was gone where the dead crabs go. Then the Sea Cow began to travel northward very slowly, stopping to hold absurd bowing councils from time to time, and Kotick followed them, saying to himself: 'People who are such idiots as these are would have been killed long ago if they hadn't found out some safe island; and what is good enough for the Sea Cow is good enough for the Sea Catch. All the same, I wish they'd hurry.'

It was weary work for Kotick. The herd never went more than forty or fifty miles a day, and stopped to feed at night, and kept close to the shore all the time; while Kotick swam round them, and over them, and under them, but he could not hurry them on one half-mile. As they went farther north they held a bowing council every few hours, and Kotick nearly bit off his moustache with impatience till he saw that they were following up a warm current of water, and then he respected them more.

One night they sank through the shiny water – sank like stones – and, for the first time he had known them, began to swim quickly. Kotick followed, and the pace astonished him, for he never dreamed that Sea Cow was anything of a swimmer. They headed for a cliff by the shore – a cliff that ran down into deep water, and plunged into a dark hole at the foot of it, twenty fathoms under the sea. It was a long, long swim, and Kotick badly wanted fresh air before he was out of the dark tunnel that they led him through.

'My wig!' he said, when he rose, gasping and puffing, into open water at the farther end. 'It was a long dive, but it was worth it.'

The sea cows had separated, and were browsing lazily along the edges of the finest beaches that Kotick had ever seen. There were long stretches of smooth-worn rock running for miles, exactly fitted to make seal-nurseries, and there were playgrounds of hard sand

sloping inland behind them, and there were rollers
for seals to dance in, and long grass to roll in, and
sand-dunes to climb up and down; and, best of all,
Kotick knew by the feel of the water, which never de-
ceives a true Sea Catch, that no men had ever come
there.

The first thing he did was to assure himself that the
fishing was good, and then he swam along the beaches
and counted up the delightful low sandy islands half
hidden in the beautiful rolling fog. Away to the northward out to sea ran a line of bars and shoals and rocks
that would never let a ship come within six miles of the
beach; and between the islands and the mainland was
a stretch of deep water that ran up to the perpen-
dicular cliffs, and somewhere below the cliffs was the
mouth of the tunnel.

'It's Novastoshnah over again, but ten times better,'
said Kotick. 'Sea Cow must be wiser than I thought.
Men can't come down the cliffs, even if there were any
men; and the shoals to seaward would knock a ship to
splinters. If any place in the sea is safe, this is it.'

He began to think of the seal he had left behind him,
but though he was in a hurry to go back to Novastoshnah, he thoroughly explored the new country, so that
he would be able to answer all questions.

Then he dived and made sure of the mouth of the
tunnel, and raced through to the southward. No one
but a sea cow or a seal would have dreamed of there
being such a place, and when he looked back at the
cliffs even Kotick could hardly believe that he had
been under them.

He was six days going home, though he was not swimming slowly; and when he hauled out just above Sea-Lion's Neck the first person he met was the seal who had been waiting for him, and she saw by the look in his eyes that he had found his island at last.

But the holluschickie and Sea Catch, his father, and all the other seals, laughed at him when he told them what he had discovered, and a young seal about his own age said: 'This is all very well, Kotick, but you can't come from no one knows where and order us off like this. Remember we've been fighting for our nurseries, and that's a thing you never did. You preferred prowling about in the sea.'

The other seals laughed at this, and the young seal began twisting his head from side to side. He had just married that year, and was making a great fuss about it.

'I've no nursery to fight for,' said Kotick. 'I want only to show you all a place where you will be safe. What's the use of fighting?'

'Oh, if you're trying to back out, of course I've no more to say,' said the young seal, with an ugly chuckle.

'Will you come with me if I win?' said Kotick; and a green light came into his eyes, for he was very angry at having to fight at all.

'Very good,' said the young seal carelessly. '*If* you win, I'll come.'

He had not time to change his mind, for Kotick's head darted out and his teeth sank in the blubber of the young seal's neck. Then he threw himself back on his haunches and hauled his enemy down the beach, shook him, and knocked him over. Then Kotick roared

72

to the seals: 'I've done my best for you these five seasons past. I've found you the island where you'll be safe, but unless your heads are dragged off your silly necks you won't believe. I'm going to teach you now. Look out for yourselves!'

Limmershin told me that never in his life – and Limmershin sees ten thousand big seals fighting every year –never in all his little life did he see anything like Kotick's charge into the nurseries. He flung himself at the biggest sea-catch he could find, caught him by the throat, choked him and bumped him and banged him till he grunted for mercy, and then threw him aside and attacked the next. You see, Kotick had never fasted for four months as the big seals did every year, and his deep-sea swimming-trips kept him in perfect condition, and, best of all, he had never fought before. His curly white mane stood up with rage, and his eyes flamed, and his big dog-teeth glistened, and he was splendid to look at.

Old Sea Catch, his father, saw him tearing past, hauling the grizzled old seals about as though they had been halibut, and upsetting the young bachelors in all directions; and Sea Catch gave one roar and shouted: 'He may be a fool, but he is the best fighter on the Beaches. Don't tackle your father, my son! He's with you!'

Kotick roared in answer, and old Sea Catch waddled in, his moustache on end, blowing like a locomotive, while Matkah and the seal that was going to marry Kotick cowered down and admired their menfolk. It was a gorgeous fight, for the two fought as long as there was a seal that dared lift up his head, and then they paraded grandly up and down the beach side by side, bellowing.

At night, just as the Northern Lights were winking and flashing through the fog, Kotick climbed a bare rock and looked down on the scattered nurseries and the torn and bleeding seals. 'Now,' he said, 'I've taught you your lesson.'

'My wig!' said old Sea Catch, boosting himself up stiffly, for he was fearfully mauled. 'The Killer Whale himself could not have cut them up worse. Son, I'm proud of you, and what's more, *I'll* come with you to your island – if there is such a place.'

'Here you, fat pigs of the sea! Who comes with me to the Sea Cow's tunnel? Answer, or I shall teach you again,' roared Kotick.

There was a murmur like the ripple of the tide all up and down the beaches. 'We will come,' said thousands of tired voices. 'We will follow Kotick, the White Seal.'

Then Kotick dropped his head between his shoulders and shut his eyes proudly. He was not a white seal any more, but red from head to tail. All the same, he would have scorned to look at or touch one of his wounds.

A week later he and his army (nearly ten thousand holluschickie and old seals) went away north to the Sea Cow's tunnel, Kotick leading them, and the seals that stayed at Novastoshnah called them idiots. But next spring when they all met off the fishing-banks of the Pacific, Kotick's seals told such tales of the new beaches beyond Sea Cow's tunnel that more and more seals left Novastoshnah.

Of course it was not all done at once, for the seals need a long time to turn things over in their minds, but year by year more seals went away from Novastoshnah, and Lukannon, and the other nurseries, to the quiet, sheltered beaches where Kotick sits all the summer through, getting bigger and fatter and stronger each year, while the holluschickie play round him, in that sea where no man comes.

ALISTAIR MACLEAN

Billy Faa and
Hector Macdonald

If you saw a stretch of upland country, flat and treeless, all boggy pools, all heather and shrubs and coarse grass with the occasional rogue boulder standing quietly by itself, you might call that stretch of country a moor. But you'd only call it that out of the kindness of your heart if you knew the Black Moss, because the Black Moss really was a moor. It lay partly in the north and partly in the west, rolling on for day after day, so bleak and huge that any traveller who dared to cross it had to keep his gaze fixed on the ground at his feet lest his eyes should stray out of his head. It was the moor of moors, the biggest and darkest and loneliest of the whole world.

There was a road through the Black Moss, a wide grassy track that flew from boundary to boundary, right down the middle without stopping, curving only as the earth curved and so long that there was sun at one end of it and snow at the other. No one knew how old this road was nor who had built it, if indeed it had been built at all. Some said that God had regretted making the moor and that not having time to unmake it he had drawn his finger down the centre of it in

76

token of cancellation. Some said that the road wasn't quite as old as that, that it was the remnant of a great prairie, squeezed in and encroached upon by the moor for century after century till only a strip was left. And some said that it was younger still, that the Romans had built it and deserted it and that it would lie there greenly rustling till armies should come again to polish it.

At any rate, there it was and by the side of it and half-way along it, propped up against the sky like the one white milestone, stood the cottage of Hector Macdonald. This cottage had belonged to Hector's father and to his grandfather and he was almost as proud of it as he was of himself. Each day as dusk fell he would step out on to the road for a look at the weather followed by a look at his house. 'I am Hector Macdonald,' he would think, 'and whether it rains or freezes I am descended from great chieftains. This is my house and it is the only house for miles and there is not a man between here and heaven that I would change places with.'

He lived in the cottage with his cat and his dog and his wife, Kirsty, and he trimmed the thatch almost as neatly as he trimmed his own whiskers and he made Kirsty polish the dishes on the shelves till each one should have the honour of reflecting his face.

Nor was this all he made her do. He kicked her out of bed every morning on to the cold floor and shouted at her till she had lit the fire and brought him his tea and toast. Every evening he made her count his gold pieces, telling them one by one then pouring them back into the iron chest while he sat listening to the music of them. 'Jingle, jingle, clink, clink.' Every night he made her climb before him into the big brass bed to warm it for him. Then he climbed in himself and put his cold feet in the middle of her back till they grew warm as well or until her back grew cold, whichever happened sooner. All the night long, till it was time for tea and toast again, he breathed in and out, quietly and neatly, one, two, one, two, and the brass rings on the end of the bed went 'jingle, jingle, clink, clink'.

On to the Black Moss one day there came a tinker called Billy Faa, a small angry man with a blackthorn stick in his right hand and a pack on his back. All the day long and sometimes all night long as well the pack went 'jingle, clink, clink', but only tools and bits of iron were in it, that he used in his trade of repairing pots and pans.

Billy Faa padded along the road for a week or two, seeking what he might devour, and presently he came to the cottage of Hector Macdonald. He stayed out of sight of anyone in it, watching it and listening to it, till night fell and Hector came out to the road as he always did. 'I am Hector Macdonald and whether it rains or freezes I am descended from great chieftains. This is my house and it is the only house for miles and there is not a man between here and heaven that I would change places with.' Then he went back into his house again, to the gold and the bed, and the sounds of 'jingle, jingle, clink, clink' rose and fell on the night air.

Billy listened in silence. When Hector had disappeared he drew the darkness a little closer around his body and stepped on to the road himself. 'And my name is Billy Faa,' he said. 'I am descended not from anything as miserable as chieftains but from the lords and earls of Little Egypt. There was a time when our servants had servants. You will change places with me, Hector Macdonald, and sooner than you think.' He shook his fist at the house and stepped back on to the moor.

For two days Billy stayed on the moor, gathering berries and pressing them and straining them and brewing from the juice of them a small bottle of Comfort. For two nights he circled Hector's house, staring at it in the darkness with his yellow eyes, drawing closer to it all the time. He saw the cat and the dog and the iron chest and the brass bed and the wife, Kirsty, and the fire and the tea and the toast every morning. When he had finished he knew the house as well as he knew the Black Moss and the desire grew in him to exchange one for the other. Very late on the second night he entered the house. He drifted among the sleeping creatures like a patch of mist and before he returned to the moor he had taken from the iron chest two gold pieces. He was ready then. On the evening of the third day he decided to pounce. 'I will try him with a limp first of all,' he thought, 'for there is no point in digging a great pit when a bit of wire snare will catch you your fool.' He came along the road just as Hector was stepping on to it. He was limping with immense authority.

'You must be the famous Hector Macdonald,' he said to Hector.

'I am descended from chieftains,' Hector answered.

'I have heard of you.'

'Yes.'

'One of my legs is dragging the other one after it.'

'I noticed that.'

'I was wondering if there was any place around here where a poor man might get shelter for the night.'

'I have not heard of such a place.'

'There's your house over there, is there not?'

'Yes, and it's the only one for miles.'

'I told you I was lame.'

'And poor as well.'

Billy sighed and took one of the gold pieces from his pocket. 'If only I could sit in front of your fire for an hour I would be a happy man,' he said.

He spun the coin in the air and Hector caught it on the way down. 'It would be cheap at twice the price,' he said to Billy. 'I am descended from chieftains.'

'You told me that already,' Billy reminded him.

'I will tell you again, too,' Hector replied, 'before your hour is up, for it is a thing that often comes into my mind.'

As they entered the house Billy took his pack off and laid it quietly down just beside the door. But he took his blackthorn stick inside with him.

When they got inside Hector pointed first to the chair at the fire, then to the clock on the wall. 'An hour soon passes,' he told Billy.

'Not for moor-dwellers,' Billy answered.

'But I am not one of those,' Hector said. He stretched himself out on the brass bed and the rings on the end of it went 'jingle, jingle, clink, clink'. He closed his eyes but kept his ears open.

Billy sat at the fire, feeling the heat creep out towards him, timidly at first but getting slowly bolder as it became used to his presence. He stood his blackthorn stick out of sight in the chimney corner, touched his pocket to see if the other gold piece and the bottle of Comfort were still there, then looked around. Near the foot of the bed he could see the iron chest with the gold in it. There was some heat coming from that, also, but not as much, he thought, as from the fire.

When he had got himself properly warmed up he switched his gaze from the room to the cat. He sat staring at it for five minutes and the cat stared back at him. 'That's a discontented-looking cat,' he thought. 'But if I had the stroking of it and the feeding of it for a week or two I'd soon change that.' Then he stared at the dog for ten minutes and the dog stared back at him. 'That's a discontented-looking dog,' he thought. 'But if I had the stroking of it and the feeding of it for a week or two I'd soon change that.' He stared last of all and longest of all at the wife, Kirsty, as she sat on her stool at the other side of the fireplace, and she stared back at him. 'That's a discontented-looking woman,' he thought. 'The most discontented-looking I have ever seen in my life. But if I had the stroking of her and the feeding of her for a week or two I'd soon change all that.'

Hector's wife and Billy Faa were still staring at one another when the clock on the wall began to chime. The bed went 'jingle, jingle, clink, clink' and Hector got up. 'An hour soon passes,' he said.

'That is true,' Billy agreed. 'Two hours would have been better.'

'Two gold pieces, also, would have been better,' said Hector.

Billy took the last gold piece from his pocket. 'I have a notion to spend my hour somewhat differently this time,' he remarked. 'I have a foolish wish to pretend to myself that I am the master of the house.'

'You could never be that,' Hector told him. 'Neither the cat nor the dog nor the wife, Kirsty, nor even the dishes on the shelves would recognize your authority. You are not descended from chieftains.'

'Well I know it,' Billy acknowledged. 'But if I was sitting here alone, with your cat and your dog and your wife, Kirsty, and you were outside wandering the Black

Moss for an hour then maybe I could persuade myself, if nobody else, that I was Hector Macdonald.'

Hector took the second gold piece and put it in his pocket. Then he took the key of the door and put that in his pocket, too. 'I will take the key with me,' he said. 'Just in case I get locked out. I have known stranger things to happen. And I have forgotten to tell you that the outside rate is more expensive. One gold piece buys you only half an hour.'

'That is a dear rate,' said Billy.

'But this is a fine house,' said Hector. 'The only one for miles. Besides, the wind is rising. It's getting to be a wild night.'

'Very well,' agreed Billy. 'Half an hour will be long enough. And just to show that I bear you no grudge and because the wind is rising I will give you a little sip of Comfort before you go. One mouthful of this will warm the ground under your feet.'

He took the bottle of Comfort from his pocket and held it up so that that it flashed and sang in the lamp-light. 'But I would not drink too much of it if I were you,' he added, 'because it is very strong and would make you dizzy.'

'I have only been made dizzy once in my life,' Hector told him.

'And when was that?' Billy asked.

'That was when Kirsty miscounted one evening and I thought one of my gold pieces was missing,' Hector replied. He took the bottle from Billy, upended it over his mouth, and drained it to the very last drop. Almost immediately he felt the fumes of the liquid uncoiling in

his stomach and beginning to claw their way upwards towards his brain. He was already becoming dizzy when he turned to the door.

'There is something else you have forgotten,' said Billy.

'What is that?' asked Hector.

'Our agreement to change clothes with one another before you went out,' Billy told him. 'How can I pretend that I am Hector Macdonald if I do not have his clothes on?'

84

'I do not remember agreeing to that,' said Hector.

'Let us settle it by asking your wife,' offered Billy. 'Kirsty, was there not such an agreement between your husband and myself?'

Kirsty stared hard at Billy Faa for a moment. Then she stared hard at her husband for a moment. Then she looked away into the fire. 'To tell you the truth,' she answered, 'I was not paying much attention.'

'There is no use asking her,' said Hector. 'She knows nothing. She has never known anything. She is not descended from chieftains as I am.'

'Nevertheless,' Kirsty remarked, 'it runs in my mind that there *was* some talk about clothes.'

'There you are,' said Billy.

'Very well, then,' said Hector. He stripped himself naked and Billy stripped himself naked and the pair of them exchanged clothes. Then Hector went out, shutting the door behind him. He looked at the clock before he went. 'Half an hour soon passes,' he said.

That is true, Billy thought. But it is also true that some half hours are longer than others. I have known them to last a lifetime. He sat down again in the big chair at the fire and first of all spoke to the cat. 'If you would call me Master,' he said to it, 'I would catch you more mice than you could eat. You would grow fat without ever leaving your own fireside. And I would stroke you till your purring filled the moor.'

'What you say about stroking is very interesting,' replied the cat. 'No one has ever stroked me enough in my whole life. But as for mice the barn is full of them. I am tired of eating mice.'

'Then I will catch you speckled trout from the pools,' said Billy. 'Fat and juicy beyond your wildest dreams. Every morning I will lay one before you. What do you say to that?'

'You are a good kind master,' the cat answered.

Billy spoke next to the dog. 'If you would call me Master,' he said to it, 'I would fetch you home more bones than you could eat. You could don roll after roll of flesh without stepping off the rug. And I would stroke you till you had to close your eyes against the pleasure of it.'

'What you say about stroking is very interesting,' replied the dog. 'No one has ever stroked me enough in my whole life. But as for bones the moor is full of them. Every day a sheep dies out there. I am tired of eating bones.'

'Then I will shoot deer for you,' said Billy. 'Fat and juicy beyond your wildest dreams. Every morning I will lay a venison steak before you. What do you say to that?'

'You are a good kind master,' the dog answered.

Billy spoke to Kirsty last of all. 'If you would call me your husband,' he said, 'I would give you half of all the gold that is in the iron chest. You could go to church on Sundays dressed so finely that no woman in the parish would dare to sit within twenty yards of you. And I would stroke you till you forgot the calendar.'

'What you say about stroking is very interesting,' replied Kirsty. 'No one has ever stroked me enough in my whole life. But as for gold, had I been the sort of woman who cares about that sort of thing I could have run away with all of it long ago. And how could I call you my husband when all the world knows you are only Billy Faa the tinker?'

'You strike a hard bargain,' Billy told her. 'So much the better. A man with gold cannot afford to have too soft a wife.'

He looked at her carefully for a long time, studying her, and she looked at the glowing peat. At last he said, 'Then I will get up every morning and light the fire for you. And I will make you tea, and toast that is crisp and crunchy beyond your wildest dreams. I will serve it to you in bed on a tray and all you will have to do will be to open your mouth. Now, what do you say to that? Will you call me your husband now?'

'What else would I call you?' asked Kirsty. 'Are you not my own dear Hector and have we not been happily wed for many years?'

'Good,' said Billy. 'Then let us go to bed, for I have had a long day and a hard day wandering the Black Moss and I am very tired.' And he took the key from his pocket and locked the door. Then he wound the clock and set it very carefully to the right time. Then he put the light out and they all went to sleep. They breathed in and out, gaily and noisily, one, two, one, two, three, and the rings on the end of the bed went 'jingle, jingle, clink, clink, clink'.

While all this was going on Hector was still out on the moor. The bottle of Comfort he had drunk was still shouting and echoing inside him and the longer he stayed the dizzier he became. Finally he could not have said whether he had been out for half an hour or half a year. 'I had better go back to my house,' he said to himself, 'and I think that is it that I see over there. At least, that is where I left it. Only I seem to remember that my house was all lit up and this one is in darkness.'

When he reached the door of the house he hunted in his pockets for the key but was unable to find it. At last he knocked.

Inside the house the dog began to bark and Billy and Kirsty woke up. 'Now, who could that be, Wife?' wondered Billy. 'Who would rouse decent folk from their sleep at this time of night?'

'I'm sure I don't know, Husband,' replied Kirsty. 'But I think it may well be a wandering tinker. You had better get up and chase him away. Take the dog with you.'

'Yes and my blackthorn stick as well,' said Billy. 'It also bites.' He got up and lit the lamp. Then he went to the door with the dog on one side of him and the stick on the other. 'Who is it?' he called.

When Hector heard himself being addressed in this fashion the surprise of it, coming after the barking of the dog, made him jump back in astonishment. His dizziness increased. 'I am Hector Macdonald,' he stammered, clutching his head. 'At least, I was when I got up this morning.'

Billy threw open the door. 'What! What!' he shouted. 'You are Billy Faa the tinker and well you know it! Play your outlandish tricks on an honest man, would you!' And he thumped Hector across the shoulders with his stick.

'But do you not remember our agreement?' Hector asked. 'We changed clothes with one another.'

'What! Someone like me, descended from great chieftains, to change clothes with a common tinker! Do you expect anyone to believe a story like that?'

'But I left here only half an hour ago,' Hector cried. 'At least, I think it was half an hour ago.'

'You lie!' Billy told him. He pointed to the clock on the wall. 'See! It is two o'clock in the morning. My wife and I have been in bed and asleep for hours. Like all decent people.'

'But I am Hector Macdonald,' Hector cried again. 'I call on heaven to witness it.'

'And I call on my cat to witness that *I* am Hector Macdonald,' replied Billy. 'Cat, who is your true master?'

The cat came over and rubbed itself against Billy's legs. But when it saw Hector it climbed up on its stilts and began spitting at him.

'And I call on my dog to witness that I am Hector Macdonald,' continued Billy. 'Dog, who is your true master?'

The dog looked up at him and banged its tail on the floor. Then it turned to Hector and growled and rumbled as loudly as if it had boulders in its throat.

'And I call on my dear wife, Kirsty, to witness that I am Hector Macdonald,' continued Billy. 'Wife, who is your true husband?'

'You are, of course, my dearest Hector,' replied Kirsty. 'Now stop arguing with that tinker and come back to bed immediately!'

Billy turned back to Hector, whose head was by now going round so fast he feared lest it should fly off his shoulders. 'Now, tinker,' he asked him, 'what is your name?'

'My name,' began Hector slowly, 'is Hector –'

Billy cut him short by thumping him yet again with the blackthorn stick. 'Be careful, now! Your name is written on the inside of your jacket. What is your name?'

Hector looked inside the jacket he was wearing. Picked out around the bottom of it in scarlet wool were the words *Billy Faa. His coat.* 'My name,' he said, 'seems to be Billy Faa.'

'A tinker name if I ever heard one,' Billy told him. 'And a bad one, too. Everybody knows the Devil was apprenticed to a Faa. Now, be off down the road before I set my stick on you again.'

Hector felt the wind still rising and the first drops of rain beginning to burn his back. 'It's a wild night,' he said.

Hector took a step towards the road. 'You've forgotten your pack,' Billy told him. He pointed to it where it still lay in the shadow beside the door.

'Why, so I have,' agreed Hector. He swung the pack up on to his shoulders. The tools and the bits of metal inside went 'jingle, jingle, clink, clink'. 'That is a familiar sound,' he added.

'Pots and pans!' Billy shouted. 'That's your trade! Pots and pans!'

Hector looked at the road, where it unwound before him. He could feel the wind pushing at his back and the pack straps settling into their old familiar grooves. His feet took a step or two of their own free will. Then another. Then another. Everything around him was scent and noise and movement. Over his head the clouds clashed and jostled and on either side of him the bog cotton glinted and the heather tossed and the myrtle flattened itself and hissed as the storm drove through it.

Between heaven and earth the road ran forward, now dipping into one element, now into the other, and wherever it led he followed. He was swinging along steadily now, his head beginning to clear. Somewhere behind him, in the gathering distance, he heard the door of the house close but he was no longer interested in that. Something was bothering him, something was missing. His body felt lighter on one side than it did on the other and presently he realized what was wrong. When he came to a blackthorn bush he stepped for a moment off the road and his fingers in the darkness ran up and down the branches like mice. When they had found him what he needed he took his jack-knife from his pocket and cut a stout stick for walking with. Then, turning up his collar and leaning well back into the wind, he set off down the road.

STEPHEN CORRIN

Bedd Gelert

In a remote little village in North Wales, a long, long time ago, there lived a prince named Llewellyn and his beautiful infant son. The mother had died in childbirth and so the prince lavished all his love and care on his only child. Prince Llewellyn also had a trusted faithful hound, named Gelert, who could sense the prince's devotion to the child and so was as protective of him as his master was, or even more so.

One morning, as the child was sleeping peacefully in its cradle, Prince Llewellyn heard the sound of a hunting horn and the barking of hunting dogs nearby.

'A share of that hunt must be mine,' he thought, 'for I am the owner of this land.' So, calling Gelert and pointing to the cradle, he simply said, 'Look after my son, while I am away,' and left. The dog obediently lay down next to the sleeping child.

Before very long the hound's fine nostrils quivered. He could scent an enemy. And indeed there was a wolf nosing in at the doorway. Gelert, quick as lightning, leaped at the beast and the next moment the two were locked in a life and death struggle. The baby went on sleeping peacefully, unaware of any danger, but the two creatures fought savagely, Gelert to protect the infant and the wolf to devour it, for it was ravenously

hungry after days of futile roaming the hills and forests.

As they fought, blood splattered all over the walls and floor, and the wolf, getting nearer the scent of its intended prey, pushed the brave dog closer to the cradle. Panting furiously, the wolf thrust Gelert right at its base and overturned it, bespattering the coverlets with blood. Miraculously, the baby continued to sleep soundly, ignorant of the mortal danger it was in and undisturbed by the ferocious growling and snarling of the two combatants. But Gelert, now sensing the imminent danger to his ward, fought back, drove his opponent to the opposite corner and sank his teeth into the wolf's throat. With a last dying snarl the wolf fell back and drew its last breath.

The faithful Gelert lay down, triumphant but exhausted, next to the sleeping child, now untidily covered by blood-stained blankets and coverlets.

About half an hour later Prince Llewellyn returned from his hunt and Gelert dragged himself to his feet and went to meet him. The prince was horrified at the sight that met his eyes, but most of all by the blood on Gelert's mouth and feet. He did not see the wolf's body in the far corner and he could only think that Gelert had killed the child.

He drew his sword and in a movement of blind fury he plunged it into the heart of his faithful hound. The dog gave a piteous and puzzled look up at his beloved master and sank back dead with a final wailing breath.

And then the prince heard a lusty cry from the direction of the cradle. He picked up the child and found it safe and sound, and then his eye fell on the torn and bloody carcass of the wolf in the corner. In a flash everything became clear.

The prince's grief was beyond control and for many years he could not erase the memory of that awful day from his guilty mind.

But if today you are on a visit to Colwyn Bay in North Wales, you can visit the village of Bedd Gelert and see the reputed grave of that famous dog, the actual spot where Prince Llewellyn is supposed to have buried his faithful companion. There is a tombstone there which tells the whole story and is headed:

TO THE MEMORY OF A BRAVE DOG.

SAKI

The Lumber Room

The children were to be driven, as a special treat, to
the sands at Jagborough. Nicholas was not to be of the
party; he was in disgrace. Only that morning he had
refused to eat his wholesome bread-and-milk on the
seemingly frivolous ground that there was a frog in it.
Older and wiser and better people had told him that
there could not possibly be a frog in his bread-and-milk
and that he was not to talk nonsense; he continued,
nevertheless, to talk what seemed the veriest nonsense,
and described with much detail the coloration and
markings of the alleged frog. The dramatic part of the
incident was that there really was a frog in Nicholas'
basin of bread-and-milk; he had put it there himself, so
he felt entitled to know something about it. The sin of
taking a frog from the garden and putting it into a
bowl of wholesome bread-and-milk was enlarged on at
great length, but the fact that stood out clearest in
the whole affair, as it presented itself to the mind of
Nicholas, was that the older, wiser, and better people
had been proved to be profoundly in error in matters
about which they had expressed the utmost assurance.

'You said there couldn't possibly be a frog in my
bread-and-milk; there was a frog in my bread-and-
milk,' he repeated, with the insistence of a skilled

tactician who does not intend to shift from favourable ground.

So his boy-cousin and girl-cousin and his quite uninteresting younger brother were to be taken to Jagborough sands that afternoon and he was to stay at home. His cousins' aunt, who insisted, by an unwarranted stretch of imagination, in styling herself his aunt also, had hastily invented the Jagborough expedition in order to impress on Nicholas the delights that he had justly forfeited by his disgraceful conduct at the breakfast-table. It was her habit, whenever one of the children fell from grace, to improvise something of a festival nature from which the offender would be rigorously debarred; if all the children sinned collectively they were suddenly informed of a circus in a neighbouring town, a circus of unrivalled merit and uncounted elephants, to which, but for their depravity, they would have been taken that very day.

A few decent tears were looked for on the part of Nicholas when the moment for the departure of the expedition arrived. As a matter of fact, however, all the crying was done by his girl-cousin, who scraped her knee rather painfully against the step of the carriage as she was scrambling in.

'How she did howl,' said Nicholas cheerfully, as the party drove off without any of the elation of high spirits that should have characterized it.

'She'll soon get over that,' said the soi-disant aunt; 'it will be a glorious afternoon for racing about over those beautiful sands. How they will enjoy themselves!'

'Bobby won't enjoy himself much, and he won't race much either,' said Nicholas with a grim chuckle; 'his boots are hurting him. They're too tight.'

'Why didn't he tell me they were hurting?' asked the aunt with some asperity.

'He told you twice, but you weren't listening. You often don't listen when we tell you important things.'

'You are not to go into the gooseberry garden,' said the aunt, changing the subject.

'Why not?' demanded Nicholas.

'Because you are in disgrace,' said the aunt loftily.

Nicholas did not admit the flawlessness of the reasoning; he felt perfectly capable of being in disgrace and in a gooseberry garden at the same moment. His face took on an expression of considerable obstinacy. It was clear to his aunt that he was determined to get into the gooseberry garden, 'only,' as she remarked to herself, 'because I have told him he is not to.'

Now the gooseberry garden had two doors by which it might be entered, and once a small person like Nicholas could slip in there he could effectually disappear from view amid the masking growth of artichokes, raspberry canes, and fruit bushes. The aunt had many other things to do that afternoon, but she spent an hour or two in trivial gardening operations among flower beds and shrubberies, whence she could keep a watchful eye on the two doors that led to the forbidden paradise. She was a woman of few ideas, with immense powers of concentration.

Nicholas made one or two sorties into the front

garden, wriggling his way with obvious stealth of purpose towards one or other of the doors, but never able for a moment to evade the aunt's watchful eye. As a matter of fact, he had no intention of trying to get into the gooseberry garden, but it was extremely convenient for him that his aunt should believe that he had; it was a belief that would keep her on self-imposed sentry-duty for the greater part of the afternoon. Having thoroughly confirmed and fortified her suspicions, Nicholas slipped back into the house and rapidly put into execution a plan of action that had long germinated in his brain. By standing on a chair in the library one could reach a shelf on which reposed a fat, important-looking key. The key was as important as it looked; it was the instrument which kept the mysteries of the lumber room secure from unauthorized intrusion, which opened a way only for aunts and such-like privileged persons. Nicholas had not had much experience of the art of fitting keys into keyholes and turning locks, but for some days past he had practised with the key of the school-room door; he did not believe in trusting too much to luck and accident. The key turned stiffly in the lock, but it turned. The door opened, and Nicholas was in an unknown land, compared with which the gooseberry garden was a stale delight, a mere material pleasure.

Often and often Nicholas had pictured to himself what the lumber room might be like, that region that was so carefully sealed from youthful eyes and concerning which no questions were ever answered. It came up

to his expectations. In the first place it was large and dimly lit, one high window opening on to the forbidden garden being its only source of illumination. In the second place it was a storehouse of unimagined treasures. The aunt-by-assertion was one of those people who think that things spoil by use and consign them to dust and damp by way of preserving them. Such parts of the house as Nicholas knew best were rather bare and cheerless, but here there were wonderful things for the eye to feast on. First and foremost there was a piece of framed tapestry that was evidently meant to be a fire-screen. To Nicholas it was a living, breathing story; he sat down on a roll of Indian hangings, glowing in wonderful colours, beneath a layer of dust, and took in all the details of the tapestry picture. A man, dressed in the hunting costume of some remote period, had just transfixed a stag with an arrow; it could not have been a difficult shot because the stag was only one or two paces away from him; in the thickly growing vegetation that the picture suggested it would not have been difficult to creep up to a feeding stag, and the two spotted dogs that were springing forward to join in the chase had evidently been trained to keep to heel till the arrow was discharged. That part of the picture was simple, if interesting, but did the huntsman see, what Nicholas saw, that four galloping wolves were coming in his direction through the wood? There might be more than four of them hidden behind the trees, and in any case would the man and his dogs be able to cope with the four wolves if they made an attack? The man had only two arrows left in his quiver, and he might miss with one or both of them; all one knew about his skill in shooting was that he could hit a large stag at a ridiculously short range. Nicholas sat for many golden minutes revolving the possibilities of the scene; he was inclined to think that there were more than four wolves and that the man and his dogs were in a tight corner.

But there were other objects of delight and interest claiming his instant attention; there were quaint twisted candlesticks in the shape of snakes, and a teapot fashioned like a china duck, out of whose open beak the tea was supposed to come. How dull and shapeless the nursery teapot seemed in comparison! And there was a carved sandalwood box packed tight with aromatic cotton-wool, and between the layers of cotton-wool were little brass figures, hump-necked bulls, and peacocks and goblins, delightful to see and to handle. Less promising in appearance was a large square book with plain black covers; Nicholas peeped into it, and, behold, it was full of coloured pictures of birds. And such birds! In the garden, and in the lanes when he went for a walk, Nicholas came across a few birds, of which the largest were an occasional magpie or wood-pigeon; here were herons and bustards, kites, toucans, tiger-bitterns, brush turkeys, ibises, golden pheasants, a whole portrait gallery of undreamed-of creatures. And as he was admiring the colouring of the mandarin duck and assigning a life-history to it, the voice of his aunt in shrill vociferation of his name came from the gooseberry garden without. She had grown suspicious of his long disappearance, and had leapt to the conclusion that he had climbed over the wall behind the sheltering screen of the lilac bushes; she was now engaged in energetic and rather hopeless search for him among the artichokes and raspberry canes.

'Nicholas, Nicholas!' she screamed, 'you are to come out of this at once. It's no use trying to hide there; I can see you all the time.'

It was probably the first time for twenty years that anyone had smiled in that lumber room.

Presently the angry repetitions of Nicholas' name gave way to a shriek, and a cry for somebody to come quickly. Nicholas shut the book, restored it carefully to its place in a corner, and shook some dust from a neighbouring pile of newspapers over it. Then he crept from the room, locked the door, and replaced the key exactly where he had found it. His aunt was still calling his name when he sauntered into the front garden.

'Who's calling?' he asked.

'Me,' came the answer from the other side of the wall; 'didn't you hear me? I've been looking for you in the gooseberry garden, and I've slipped into the rain-water tank. Luckily there's no water in it, but the sides are slippery and I can't get out. Fetch the little ladder from under the cherry tree –'

'I was told I wasn't to go into the gooseberry garden,' said Nicholas promptly.

'I told you not to, and now I tell you that you may,' came the voice from the rain-water tank, rather impatiently.

'Your voice doesn't sound like aunt's,' objected Nicholas; 'you may be the Evil One tempting me to be disobedient. Aunt often tells me that the Evil One tempts me and that I always yield. This time I'm not going to yield.'

'Don't talk nonsense,' said the prisoner in the tank; 'go and fetch the ladder.'

'Will there be strawberry jam for tea?' asked Nicholas innocently.

'Certainly there will be,' said the aunt, privately resolving that Nicholas should have none of it.

'Now I know that you are the Evil One and not aunt,' shouted Nicholas gleefully; 'when we asked aunt for strawberry jam yesterday she said there wasn't any.

I know there are four jars of it in the store cupboard, because I looked, and of course you know it's there, but she doesn't, because she said there wasn't any. Oh, Devil, you have sold yourself!'

There was an unusual sense of luxury in being able to talk to an aunt as though one was talking to the Evil One, but Nicholas knew, with childish discernment, that such luxuries were not to be over-indulged in. He walked noisily away, and it was a kitchenmaid, in search of parsley, who eventually rescued the aunt from the rain-water tank.

Tea that evening was partaken of in a fearsome silence. The tide had been at its highest when the children had arrived at Jagborough Cove, so there had been no sands to play on – a circumstance that the aunt had overlooked in the haste of organizing her punitive expedition. The tightness of Bobby's boots had had a disastrous effect on his temper the whole of the afternoon, and altogether the children could not have been said to have enjoyed themselves. The aunt maintained the frozen muteness of one who has suffered undignified and unmerited detention in a rain-water tank for thirty-five minutes. As for Nicholas, he, too, was silent, in the absorption of one who has much to think about; it was just possible, he considered, that the huntsman would escape with his hounds while the wolves feasted on the stricken stag.

The Minotaur

In the old city of Troezene, at the foot of a lofty mountain, there lived, a very long time ago, a little boy named Theseus. His grandfather, King Pittheus, was the sovereign of that country, and was reckoned a very wise man; so that Theseus, being brought up in the royal palace, and being naturally a bright lad, could hardly fail of profiting by the old king's instructions. His mother's name was Aethra. As for his father, the boy had never seen him. But from his earliest remembrance, Aethra used to go with little Theseus into a wood, and sit down upon a moss-grown rock, which was deeply sunken into the earth. Here she often talked with her son about his father, and said that he was called Aegeus, and that he was a great king, and ruled over Attica, and dwelt at Athens, which was as famous a city as any in the world. Theseus was very fond of hearing about King Aegeus, and often asked his good mother Aethra why he did not come and live with them at Troezene.

'Ah, my dear son,' answered Aethra, with a sigh, 'a monarch has his people to take care of. The men and women over whom he rules are in the place of children to him; and he can seldom spare time to love his own children as other parents do. Your father will never be able to leave his kingdom for the sake of seeing his little boy.'

'Well, but, dear mother,' asked the boy, 'why cannot I go to this famous city of Athens, and tell King Aegeus that I am his son?'

'That may happen by and by,' said Aethra. 'Be patient, and we shall see. You are not yet big enough and strong enough to set out on such an errand.'

'And how soon shall I be strong enough?' Theseus persisted in inquiring.

'You are but a tiny boy as yet,' replied his mother. 'See if you can lift this rock on which we are sitting.'

The little fellow had a great opinion of his own strength. So, grasping the rough protuberances of the rock, he tugged and toiled amain and got himself quite out of breath, without being able to stir the heavy stone. It seemed to be rooted into the ground. No wonder he could not move it; for it would have taken all the force of a very strong man to lift it out of its earthy bed. His mother stood looking on, with a sad kind of smile on her lips and in her eyes to see the zealous and yet puny efforts of her boy. She could not help being sorrowful at finding him already so impatient to begin his adventures in the world.

'You see how it is, my dear Theseus,' said she. 'You must possess far more strength than now before I can trust you to go to Athens, and tell King Aegeus that you are his son. But when you can lift this rock, and show me what is hidden beneath it, I promise you my permission to depart.'

Often and often, after this, did Theseus ask his mother whether it was time for him to go to Athens; and still his mother pointed to the rock, and told him that, for years to come, he could not be strong enough to move it. And again and again the rosy-cheeked and curly-headed boy would tug and strain at the huge mass of stone, striving, child as he was, to do what a giant could hardly have done without taking both of his great hands to the task. Meanwhile the rock seemed to be sinking farther and farther into the ground. The moss grew over it thicker and thicker until at last it looked almost like a soft green seat, with only a few knobs of granite peeping out. The overhanging trees also shed their brown leaves upon it, as often as the autumn came; and at its base grew ferns and wild flowers, some of which crept quite over its surface. To all appearance the rock was as firmly fastened as any other portion of the earth's substance.

But, difficult as the matter looked, Theseus was now growing up to be such a vigorous youth that, in his own opinion, the time would quickly come when he might hope to get the upper hand of this ponderous lump of stone.

'Mother, I do believe it has started!' cried he, after one of his attempts. 'The earth around it is certainly a little cracked!'

'No, no, child!' his mother hastily answered. 'It is not possible you can have moved it, such a boy as you still are!'

Nor would she be convinced, although Theseus showed her the place where he fancied that the stem of

a flower had been partly uprooted by the movement of
the rock. But Aethra sighed and looked disquieted; for,
no doubt, she began to be conscious that her son was
no longer a child, and that, in a little while hence, she
must send him forth among the perils and troubles of
the world.

It was not more than a year afterwards when they
were again sitting on the moss-covered stone. Aethra
had once more told him the oft-repeated story of his
father, and how gladly he would receive Theseus at his
stately palace, and how he would present him to his
courtiers and the people, and tell them that here was
the heir of his dominions. The eyes of Theseus glowed
with enthusiasm, and he would hardly sit still to hear
his mother speak.

'Dear mother Aethra,' he exclaimed, 'I never felt
half so strong as now! I am no longer a child, nor a
boy, nor a mere youth! I feel myself a man! It is now
time to make one earnest trial to remove the stone.'

'Ah, my dearest Theseus,' replied his mother, 'not
yet! not yet!'

'Yes, mother,' said he, resolutely, 'the time has come!'

Then Theseus bent himself in good earnest to the
task, and strained every sinew, with manly strength
and resolution. He put his whole brave heart into the
effort. He wrestled with the big and sluggish stone as if
it had been a living enemy. He heaved, he lifted, he
resolved now to succeed, or else to perish there, and let
the rock be his monument forever! Aethra stood gazing
at him, and clasped her hands, partly with a mother's
pride, and partly with a mother's sorrow. The great

rock stirred! Yes, it was raised slowly from the bedded moss and earth, uprooting the shrubs and flowers along with it, and was turned upon its side. Theseus had conquered!

While taking breath, he looked joyfully at his mother, and she smiled upon him through her tears.

'Yes, Theseus,' she said, 'the time has come, and you must stay no longer at my side! See what King Aegeus, your royal father, left for you, beneath the stone, when he lifted it in his mighty arms, and laid it on the spot whence you have now removed it.'

Theseus looked, and saw that the rock had been placed over another slab of stone, containing a cavity within it; so that it somewhat resembled a roughly made chest or coffer of which the upper mass had served as the lid. Within the cavity lay a sword, with a golden hilt, and a pair of sandals.

'That was your father's sword,' said Aethra, 'and those were his sandals. When he went to be King of Athens, he bade me treat you as a child until you should prove yourself a man by lifting this heavy stone. This task being accomplished, you are to put on his sandals, in order to follow in your father's footsteps, and to gird on his sword, so that you may fight giants and dragons, as King Aegeus did in his youth.'

'I will set out for Athens this very day!' cried Theseus.

But his mother persuaded him to stay a day or two longer, while she got ready some necessary articles for his journey. When his grandfather, the wise King Pittheus, heard that Theseus intended to present himself at his father's palace, he earnestly advised him to get on board of a vessel, and go by sea; because he might thus arrive within fifteen miles of Athens, without either fatigue or danger.

'The roads are very bad by land,' quoth the venerable king; 'and they are terribly infested with robbers and monsters. A mere lad like Theseus is not fit to be trusted on such a perilous journey all by himself. No, no; let him go by sea!'

But when Theseus heard of robbers and monsters, he pricked up his ears, and was so much the more eager to take the road, along which they were to be met with. On the third day, therefore, he bade a respectful farewell to his grandfather, thanking him for all his kindness; and after affectionately embracing his mother, he set forth, with a good many of her tears glistening on his cheeks, and some, if the truth must be told, that gushed out of his own eyes. But he let the sun and wind dry them, and walked stoutly on, playing with the golden hilt of his sword, and taking very manly strides in his father's sandals.

I cannot stop to tell you hardly any of the adventures that befell Theseus on the road to Athens. It is enough to say that he quite cleared that part of the country of the robbers, about whom King Pittheus had been so much alarmed. One of these bad people was named Procrustes; and he was indeed a terrible fellow, and had an ugly way of making fun of the poor travellers who happened to fall into his clutches. In his cavern he had a bed, on which, with great pretence of hospitality, he invited his guests to lie down; but if they happened to be shorter than the bed, this wicked villain stretched them out by main force; or, if they were too tall, he lopped off their heads or feet, and laughed at what he had done as an excellent joke. Thus, however weary a man might be, he never liked to lie in the bed of Procrustes. Another of these robbers, named Scinis, must likewise have been a very great scroundrel. He was in the habit of flinging his victims off a high cliff into the sea; and, in order to give him exactly his deserts, Theseus tossed him off the very same place. But if you will believe me, the sea would not pollute itself by receiving such a bad person into its bosom, neither would the earth, having once got rid of him, consent to take him back; so that, between the cliff and the sea, Scinis stuck fast in the air, which was forced to bear the burden of his naughtiness.

After these memorable deeds, Theseus heard of an enormous sow, which ran wild, and was the terror of all the farmers round about; and, as he did not consider himself above doing any good thing that came in his way, he killed this monstrous creature, and gave the carcass to the poor people for bacon. The great sow had been an awful beast while ramping about the woods and fields, but was a pleasant object enough when cut up into joints, and smoking on I know not how many dinner-tables.

Thus, by the time he reached his journey's end, Theseus had done many valiant feats with his father's golden-hilted sword, and had gained the renown of being one of the bravest young men of the day. His fame travelled faster than he did, and reached Athens before him. As he entered the city, he heard the inhabitants talking at the street corner and saying that Hercules was brave, and Jason too, and Castor and Pollux likewise, but that Theseus, the son of their own king, would turn out as great a hero as the best of them. Theseus took longer strides on hearing this, and fancied himself sure of a magnificent reception at his father's court, since he came thither with Fame to blow her trumpet before him, and cry to King Aegeus, 'Behold your son.'

He little suspected, innocent youth that he was, that here in this very Athens, where his father reigned, a greater danger awaited him than any which he had encountered on the road. Yet this was the truth. You must understand that the father of Theseus, though not very old in years, was almost worn out with the cares of government, and had thus grown aged before his time. His nephews, not expecting him to live a very great while, intended to get all the power of the kingdom into their own hands. But when they heard that Theseus had arrived in Athens, and learned what a gallant young man he was, they saw that he would not be at all the kind of person to let them steal away his father's crown and sceptre, which ought to be his own by right of inheritance. Thus these bad-hearted nephews of King Aegeus, who were the own cousins of Theseus, at once became his enemies. A still more dangerous enemy was Medea, the wicked enchantress; for she was now the king's wife, and wanted to give the kingdom to her son Medus, instead of letting it be given to the son of Aethra, whom she hated.

It so happened that the king's nephews met Theseus, and found out who he was, just as he reached the entrance of the royal palace. With all their evil designs against him, they pretended to be their cousin's best friends, and expressed great joy at making his acquaintance. They proposed to him that he should come into the king's presence as a stranger, in order to try whether Aegeus would discover in the young man's features any likeness either to himself or his mother Aethra, and thus recognize him for a son. Theseus consented; for he fancied that his father would know him in a moment, by the love that was in his heart. But while he waited at the door, the nephews ran and told King Aegeus that a young man had arrived in Athens, who, to their certain knowledge, intended to put him to death, and get possession of his royal crown.

'And he is now waiting for admission to your Majesty's presence,' added they.

'Aha!' cried the old king, on hearing this. 'Why, he must be a very wicked young fellow indeed! Pray, what would you advise me to do with him?'

In reply to this question, the wicked Medea put in her word. As I have already told you, she was a famous enchantress. According to some stories, she was in the habit of boiling old people in a large cauldron, under pretence of making them young again; but King Aegeus, I suppose, did not fancy such an uncomfortable way of growing young, or perhaps was contented to be old, and therefore would never let himself be popped into the cauldron. If there were time to spare from more important matters, I should be glad to tell you of Medea's fiery chariot, drawn by winged dragons, in which the enchantress used often to take an airing among the clouds. This chariot, in fact, was the vehicle that first brought her to Athens, where she had done nothing but mischief ever since her arrival.

But these and many other wonders must be left untold; and it is enough to say that Medea, among a thousand other bad things, knew how to prepare a poison that was instantly fatal to whomsoever might so much as touch it with his lips.

So when the king asked what he should do with Theseus, this naughty woman had an answer ready at her tongue's end.

'Leave that to me, please your Majesty,' she replied. 'Only admit this evil-minded young man to your presence, treat him civilly, and invite him to drink a goblet of wine. Your Majesty is well aware that I sometimes amuse myself with distilling very powerful medicines. Here is one of them in this small phial. As to what it is made of, that is one of my secrets of state. Do but let me put a single drop into the goblet, and let the young man taste it; and I will answer for it he shall quite lay aside the bad designs with which he comes hither.'

As she said this, Medea smiled; but for all her smiling face, she meant nothing less than to poison the poor innocent Theseus before his father's eyes. And King Aegeus, like most other kings, thought any punishment mild enough for a person who was accused of plotting against his life. He therefore made little or no objection to Medea's scheme, and as soon as the poisonous wine was ready gave orders that the young stranger should be admitted into his presence. The goblet was set on a table beside the king's throne; and a fly, meaning just to sip a little from the brim, immediately tumbled into it dead. Observing this, Medea looked round at the nephews, and smiled again.

When Theseus was ushered into the royal apartment, the only object that he seemed to behold was the white-bearded old king. There he sat on his magnificent throne, a dazzling crown on his head, and sceptre in his hand. His aspect was stately and majestic, although his years and infirmities weighed heavily upon him as if each year were a lump of lead, and each infirmity a ponderous stone, and all were bundled up together, and laid upon his weary shoulders. The tears both of joy and sorrow sprang into the young man's eyes; for he thought how sad it was to see his dear father so infirm, and how sweet it would be to support him with his own youthful strength, and to cheer him up with the alacrity of his loving spirit. When a son takes his father into his warm heart, it renews the old man's youth in a better way than by the heat of Medea's magic cauldron. And this was what Theseus resolved to do. He could scarcely wait to see whether King Aegeus would recognize him, so eager was he to throw himself into his arms.

Advancing to the foot of the throne, he attempted to make a little speech, which he had been thinking about as he came up the stairs. But he was almost choked by a great many tender feelings that gushed out of his heart and swelled into his throat, all struggling to find utterance together. And therefore, unless he could have laid his full over-brimming heart into the king's hand, poor Theseus knew not what to do or say. The cunning Medea observed what was passing in the young man's mind. She was more wicked at that moment than ever she had been before; for (and it makes me tremble to tell you of it) she did her worst to turn all this unspeakable love with which Theseus was agitated to his own ruin and destruction.

'Does your Majesty see his confusion?' she whispered in the king's ear. 'He is so conscious of guilt, that he trembles and cannot speak. The wretch lives too long! Quick, offer him the wine!'

Now King Aegeus had been gazing earnestly at the young stranger as he drew near the throne. There was something he knew not what, either in his white brow, or in the fine expression of his mouth, or in his beautiful and tender eyes, that made him indistinctly feel as if he had seen this youth before; as if, indeed, he had trotted him on his knee when a baby, and had beheld him growing to be a stalwart man, while he himself grew old. But Medea guessed how the king felt, and would not suffer him to yield to these natural sensibilities; although they were the voice of his deeper heart, telling him, as plainly as it could speak, that there was his dear son, and Aethra's son, coming to claim him for a father. The enchantress again whispered in the king's ear, and compelled him, by her witchcraft, to see everything under a false aspect.

He made up his mind, therefore, to let Theseus drink of the poisoned wine.

'Young man,' said he, 'you are welcome! I am proud

to show hospitality to so heroic a youth. Do me the favour to drink the contents of this goblet. It is brimming over, as you see, with delicious wine; such I bestow only on those who are worthy of it. None is more worthy to quaff it than yourself!'

So saying, King Aegeus took the golden goblet from the table, and was about to offer it to Theseus. But partly through his infirmities, and partly because it seemed so sad a thing to take away this young man's life, however wicked he might be, and partly, no doubt, because his heart was wiser than his head, and quaked within him at the thought of what he was going to do – for all these reasons, the king's hand trembled so much that a great deal of the wine slopped over. In order to strengthen his purpose, and fearing lest the whole of the precious poison should be wasted, one of his nephews now whispered to him,

'Has your Majesty any doubt of this stranger's guilt? There is the very sword with which he meant to slay you. How sharp, and bright, and terrible it is! Quick! – let him taste the wine, or perhaps he may do the deed even yet.'

At these words, Aegeus drove every thought and feeling out of his breast, except the one idea of how justly the young man deserved to be put to death. He sat erect on his throne, and held out the goblet of wine with a steady hand, and bent on Theseus a frown of kingly severity; for all, he had too noble a spirit to murder even a treacherous enemy with a deceitful smile upon his face.

'Drink!' said he, in the stern tone with which he was

wont to condemn a criminal to be beheaded. 'You have well deserved of me such wine as this!'

Theseus held out his hand to take the wine. But, before he touched it, King Aegeus trembled again. His eye had fallen on the gold-hilted sword that hung at the young man's side. He drew back the goblet.

'That sword!' he cried; 'how came you by it?'

'It was my father's sword,' replied Theseus, with a tremulous voice. 'These were his sandals. My dear mother (her name is Aethra) told me his story while I grew yet a child. But it is only a month since I grew strong enough to lift the heavy stone, and take the sword and sandals from beneath it, and come to Athens, to seek my father.'

'My son! my son!' cried King Aegeus, flinging away the fatal goblet, and tottering down from the throne to fall into the arms of Theseus. 'Yes, these are Aethra's eyes. It is my son.'

I have forgotten what became of the king's nephews. But when the wicked Medea saw this new turn of affairs, she hurried out of the room, and going to her private chamber, lost no time in setting her enchantments to work. In a few moments, she heard a great noise of hissing snakes outside of the chamber window; and, behold! there was her fiery chariot, and four huge winged serpents, wriggling and twisting in the air, flourishing their tails higher than the top of the palace, and all ready to set off on an aerial journey. Medea stayed only long enough to take her son with her, and to steal the crown jewels, together with the king's best robes, and whatever other valuable things she could lay hands on; and getting into the chariot she whipped up the snakes, and ascended high over the city.

The king, hearing the hiss of the serpents, scrambled as fast as he could to the window, and bawled out to the abominable enchantress never to come back. The whole people of Athens, too, who had run out of doors to see this wonderful spectacle, set up a shout of joy at the prospect of getting rid of her. Medea, almost bursting with rage, uttered precisely such a hiss as one of her own snakes, only ten times more venomous and spiteful; and glaring fiercely out of the blaze of the chariot, she shook her hands over the multitude below, as if she were scattering a million curses among them. In so doing, however, she unintentionally let fall about five hundred diamonds of the first water, together with a thousand great pearls, and two thousand emeralds, rubies, sapphires, opals, and topazes, to which she had helped herself out of the king's strongbox. All these came pelting down, like a shower of many-coloured hailstones, upon the heads of grown people and children, who forthwith gathered them up, and carried them back to the palace. But King Aegeus told them they were welcome to the whole, and to twice as many more, if he had them, for the sake of his delight at finding his son and losing the wicked Medea. And, indeed, if you had seen how hateful was her last look, as the flaming chariot flew upward, you would not have wondered that both king and people should think her departure a good riddance.

And now Prince Theseus was taken into great favour by his royal father. The old king was never weary of having him sit beside him on his throne (which was quite wide enough for two), and of hearing him tell about his dear mother, and his childhood, and his many boyish efforts to lift the ponderous stone. Theseus, however, was much too brave and active a young man to be willing to spend all his time in relating things which had already happened. His ambition was to perform other and more heroic deeds, which should be better worth telling in prose and verse. Nor had he been long in Athens before he caught and chained a terrible mad bull, and made a public show of him, greatly to the wonder and admiration of good King Aegeus and his subjects. But pretty soon he undertook an affair that made all his foregone adventures seem like mere boy's play. The occasion of it was as follows:

One morning, when Prince Theseus awoke, he fancied that he must have had a very sorrowful dream, and that it was still running in his mind, even now that his eyes were open. For it appeared as if the air was full of a melancholy wail; and when he listened more attentively, he could hear sobs and groans, and screams of woe, mingled with deep, quiet sighs, which came from the king's palace, and from the streets, and from the temples, and from every habitation in the city. And all these mournful noises, issuing out of thousands of separate hearts, united themselves into the one great sound of affliction which had startled Theseus from slumber. He put on his clothes as quickly as he could (not forgetting his sandals and gold-hilted sword), and hastening to the king inquired what it all meant.

'Alas! my son,' quoth King Aegeus, heaving a long sigh, 'here is a very lamentable matter in hand! This is the woefullest anniversary in the whole year. It is the day when we annually draw lots to see which of the youths and maidens of Athens shall go to be devoured by the horrible Minotaur!'

'The Minotaur!' exclaimed Prince Theseus; and like a brave young prince as he was, he put his hand to the hilt of his sword. 'What kind of a monster may that be? Is it not possible, at the risk of one's life, to slay him?'

But King Aegeus shook his venerable head, and to convince Theseus that it was quite a hopeless case, he gave him an explanation of the whole affair. It seems that in the island of Crete there lived a certain dreadful monster, called a Minotaur, which was shaped partly like a man and partly like a bull, and was altogether such a hideous sort of a creature that it is really disagreeable to think of him. If he were suffered to exist at all, it should have been on some desert island, or in the duskiness of some deep cavern, where nobody would ever be tormented by his abominable aspect. But King Minos, who reigned over Crete, laid out a vast deal of money in building a habitation for the Minotaur, and took great care of his health and comfort, merely for mischief's sake. A few years before this time, there had been a war between the city of Athens and the island of Crete, in which the Athenians were beaten, and compelled to beg for peace. No peace could they obtain, however, except on condition that they should send seven young men and seven maidens every year to be devoured by the monster of the cruel King Minos. For three years past, this grievous calamity had been borne. And the sobs, and groans, and shrieks, with which the city was now filled, were caused by the people's woe, because the fatal day had come again, when the fourteen victims were to be chosen by lot; and the old people feared lest their sons or daughters might be taken, and the youths and damsels dreaded lest they themselves might be destined to glut the ravenous maw of that detestable man-brute.

But when Theseus heard the story, he straightened himself up so that he seemed taller than ever before; and as for his face, it was indignant, despiteful, bold, tender, and compassionate, all in one look.

'Let the people of Athens, this year, draw lots for only six young men, instead of seven,' said he. 'I will myself be the seventh; and let the Minotaur devour me if he can!'

'O my dear son,' cried King Aegeus, 'why should you expose yourself to this horrible fate? You are a royal prince, and have a right to hold yourself above the destinies of common men.'

'It is because I am a prince, your son, and the rightful heir of your kingdom, that I freely take upon me the calamity of your subjects,' answered Theseus. 'And you, my father, being king over this people and answerable to Heaven for their welfare, are bound to sacrifice what is dearest to you, rather than the son or daughter of the poorest citizen should come to any harm.'

The old king shed tears, and besought Theseus not to leave him desolate in his old age, more especially as he had just begun to know the happiness of possessing a good and valiant son. Theseus, however, felt he was in the right, and therefore would not give up his resolution. But he assured his father that he did not intend to be eaten up, unresistingly, like a sheep, and that, if the Minotaur devoured him, it should not be without a battle for his dinner. And finally, since he could not help it, King Aegeus consented to let him go. So a vessel was got ready, and rigged with black sails; and Theseus, with six other young men and seven tender and beautiful damsels, came down to the harbour to embark. A sorrowful multitude accompanied them to the shore. There was the poor old king, leaning on his son's arm, and looking as if his single heart held all the grief of Athens. Just as Prince Theseus was going on board, his father bethought himself of one last word to say.

'My beloved son,' said he, grasping the prince's hand, 'you observe that the sails of this vessel are black; as indeed they ought to be, since it goes on a voyage of sorrow and despair. Now, being weighed down with infirmities, I know not whether I can survive till the vessel shall return. But, as long as I do live, I shall creep daily to the top of yonder cliff, to watch if there be a sail upon the sea. And, dearest Theseus, if by some happy chance you should escape the jaws of the Minotaur, then tear down those dismal sails, and hoist others that shall be bright as the sunshine. Beholding them on the horizon, myself and all the people will know that you are coming back victorious, and will welcome you with such a festal uproar as Athens never heard before.'

Theseus promised that he would do so. Then, going on board, the mariners trimmed the vessel's black sails to the wind, which blew faintly off the shore, being pretty much made up of the sighs that everybody kept pouring forth on this melancholy occasion. But by and by, when they had got fairly out to sea, there came a stiff breeze from the north-west, and drove them along as merrily over the white-capped waves as if they had been going on the most delightful errand imaginable. And though it was a sad business enough, I rather question whether fourteen young people, without any old persons to keep them in order, could continue to spend the whole time of the voyage in being miserable. There had been some few dances upon the undulating deck, I suspect, and some hearty bursts of laughter, and other such unseasonable merriments among the victims, before the high blue mountains of Crete began to show themselves among the far-off clouds. That sight, to be sure, made them all very grave again.

Theseus stood among the sailors gazing eagerly towards the land; although, as yet, is seemed hardly more substantial than the clouds amidst which the mountains were looming up. Once or twice he fancied that he saw a glare of some bright object, a long way off, flinging a gleam across the waves.

'Did you see that flash of light?' he inquired of the master of the vessel.

'No, prince; but I have seen it before,' answered the master. 'It came from Talus, I suppose.'

As the breeze became fresher just then, the master was busy with trimming his sails, and had no more time to answer questions. But while the vessel flew faster and faster towards Crete, Theseus was astonished to behold a human figure, gigantic in size, which appeared to be striding with a measured movement along the margin of the island. It stepped from cliff to cliff, and sometimes from one headland to another, while the sea foamed and thundered on the shore beneath, and dashed its jets of spray over the giant's feet. What was still more remarkable, whenever the sun shone on this huge figure, it flickered and glimmered; its vast countenance, too, had a metallic lustre, and threw great flashes of splendour through the air. The folds of its garments, moreover, instead of waving in the wind, fell heavily over its limbs, as if woven of some kind of metal.

The nigher the vessel came, the more Theseus wondered what this immense giant could be, and whether it actually had life or no. For, although it walked, and made other life-like motions, there yet was a kind of jerk in its gait which, together with its brazen aspect, caused the young prince to suspect that it was no true giant, but only a wonderful piece of machinery. The figure looked all the more terrible because it carried an enormous brass club on its shoulder.

'What is this wonder?' Theseus asked of the master of the vessel, who was now at leisure to answer him.

'It is Talus, the Man of Brass,' said the master.

'And is he a live giant or a brazen image?' asked Theseus.

'That, truly,' replied the master, 'is the point which has always perplexed me. Some say, indeed, that this Talus was hammered out for the King Minos by

Vulcan himself, skilfullest of all workers in metal. But who ever saw a brazen image that had sense enough to walk round an island three times a day, as this giant walks round the island of Crete, challenging every vessel that comes nigh the shore? And, on the other hand, what living thing, unless his sinews were made of brass, would not be weary of marching eighteen hundred miles in the twenty-four hours, as Talus does, without ever sitting down to rest? He is a puzzler, take him how you will.'

Still the vessel went bounding onward; and now Theseus could hear the brazen clangour of the giant's footsteps, as he trod heavily upon the sea-beaten rocks, some of which were seen to crack and crumble into the foamy waves beneath his weight. As they approached the entrance of the port, the giant straddled clear across it, with a foot firmly planted on each headland, and uplifting his club to such a height that its butt-end was hidden in a cloud, he stood in that formidable posture, with the sun gleaming all over his metallic face. There seemed nothing else to be expected but that, the next moment, he would fetch his great club down, slam bang, and smash the vessel into a thousand pieces without heeding how many innocent people he might destroy; for there is seldom any mercy in a giant, you know, and quite as little in a piece of brass clockwork. But just when Theseus and his companions thought the blow was coming, the brazen lips unclosed themselves, and the figure spoke.

'Whence come you, strangers?'

And when the ringing voice ceased, there was just

such a reverberation as you may have heard within a great church bell, for a moment or two after the stroke of the hammer.

'From Athens!' shouted the master in reply.

'On what errand?' thundered the Man of Brass. And he whirled his club aloft more threateningly than ever, as if he were about to smite them with a thunder-stroke right amidships, because Athens, so little while ago, had been at war with Crete.

'We bring the seven youths and the seven maidens,' answered the master, 'to be devoured by the Minotaur!'

'Pass!' cried the brazen giant.

That one loud word rolled all about the sky while again there was a booming reverberation within the figure's breast. The vessel glided between the headlands of the port, and the giant resumed his march. In a few moments, this wondrous sentinel was far away, flashing in the distant sunshine, and revolving with immense strides around the island of Crete, as it was his never-ceasing task to do.

No sooner had they entered the harbour than a party of the guards of King Minos came down to the waterside, and took charge of the fourteen young men and damsels. Surrounded by these armed warriors, Prince Theseus and his companions were led to the king's palace, and ushered into his presence. Now, Minos was a stern and pitiless king. If the figure that guarded Crete was made of brass, then the monarch, who ruled over it, might be thought to have a still harder metal in his breast, and might have been called a man of iron. He bent his shaggy brows upon the poor Athenian victims. Any other mortal, beholding their fresh and tender beauty and their innocent looks, would have felt himself sitting on thorns until he had made every soul of them happy, by bidding them go free as the summer wind. But this immitigable Minos cared only to examine whether they were plump enough to satisfy the Minotaur's appetite. For my part, I wish he himself had been the only victim; and the monster would have found him a pretty tough one.

One after another, King Minos called these pale frightened youths and sobbing maidens to his footstool, gave them each a poke in the ribs with his sceptre (to try whether they were in good flesh or no), and dismissed them with a nod to his guards. But when his eyes rested on Theseus, the king looked at him more attentively, because his face was calm and brave.

'Young man,' asked he, with his stern voice, 'are you not appalled at the certainty of being devoured by this terrible Minotaur?'

'I have offered my life in a good cause,' answered Theseus, 'and therefore I give it freely and gladly. But thou, King Minos, art thou not thyself appalled, who, year after year, hast perpetrated this deadful wrong, by giving seven innocent youths and as many maidens to be devoured by a monster? Dost thou not tremble, wicked king, to turn thine eyes inward on thine own heart? Sitting there on thy golden throne, and in thy robes of majesty, I tell thee to thy face, King Minos, thou art a more hideous monster than the Minotaur himself!'

'Aha! do you think me so?' cried the king, laughing in his cruel way. 'Tomorrow, at breakfast time, you shall have an opportunity of judging which is the greater monster, the Minotaur or the king. Take them away, guards; and let this free-spoken youth be the Minotaur's first morsel!'

Near the king's throne (though I had no time to tell you so before) stood his daughter Ariadne. She was a beautiful and tender-hearted maiden, and looked at these poor doomed captives with very different feelings from those of the iron-breasted King Minos. She really wept, indeed, at the idea of how much human happiness would be needlessly thrown away, by giving so many young people, in the first bloom and rose blossom of their lives, to be eaten up by a creature who, no doubt, would have preferred a fat ox, or even a large pig, to the plumpest of them. And when she beheld the brave-spirited figure of Prince Theseus bearing himself so calmly in his terrible peril, she grew a hundred times more pitiful than before. As the guards were taking him away, she flung herself at the king's feet, and besought him to set all the captives free, and especially this one young man.

'Peace, foolish girl!' answered King Minos. 'What hast thou to do with an affair like this? It is a matter of state policy, and therefore quite beyond thy weak comprehension. Go water thy flowers, and think no more of these Athenian caitiffs, whom the Minotaur shall as certainly eat up for breakfast as I will eat a partridge for my supper.'

So saying, the king looked cruel enough to devour

Theseus and all the rest of the captives himself, had
there been no Minotaur to save him the trouble. As he
would hear not another word in their favour, the pris-
oners were now led away, and clapped into a dungeon,
where the jailer advised them to sleep as soon as possible, because the Minotaur was in the habit of calling
for breakfast early. The seven maidens and six of the
young men soon sobbed themselves to slumber. But
Theseus was not like them. He felt conscious that he

was wiser, and braver, and stronger than his companions, and that therefore he had the responsibility of all their lives upon him, and must consider whether there was no way to save them, even in this last extremity. So he kept himself awake, and paced to and fro across the gloomy dungeon in which they were shut up.

Just before midnight the door was softly unbarred, and the gentle Ariadne showed herself, with a torch in her hand. 'Are you awake, Prince Theseus?' she whispered.

'Yes,' answered Theseus. 'With so little time to live, I do not choose to waste any of it in sleep.'

'Then follow me,' said Ariadne, 'and tread softly.'

What had become of the jailer and the guards, Theseus never knew. But, however that might be, Ariadne opened all the doors, and led him forth from the darksome prison into the pleasant moonlight.

'Theseus,' said the maiden, 'you can now get on board your vessel, and sail away from Crete.'

'No,' answered the young man; 'I will never leave Crete unless I can first slay the Minotaur, and save my poor companions, and deliver Athens from this cruel tribute.'

'I knew that would be your resolution,' said Ariadne. 'Come, then, with me, brave Theseus. Here is your own sword, which the guards deprived you of. You will need it; and pray Heaven you may use it well.'

Then she led Theseus along by the hand until they came to a dark, shadowy grove, where the moonlight wasted itself on the tops of the trees, without shedding hardly so much as a glimmering beam upon their pathway. After going a good way through this obscurity they reached a high marble wall, which was overgrown with creeping plants that made it shaggy with their verdure. The wall seemed to have no door nor any windows, but rose up lofty, and massive, and mysterious, and was neither to be clambered over nor, so far as Theseus could perceive, to be passed through. Nevertheless, Ariadne did press one of her soft little fingers against a particular block of marble, and, though it looked as solid as any other part of the wall, it yielded to her touch, disclosing an entrance just wide enough to admit them. They crept through, and the marble swung back into its place.

'We are now,' said Ariadne, 'in the famous labyrinth which Daedalus built before he made himself a pair of wings, and flew away from our island like a bird. That Daedalus was a very cunning workman; but of all his artful contrivances, this labyrinth is the most wondrous. Were we to take but a few steps from the doorway, we might wander about all our lifetime, and never find it again. Yet in the very centre of this labyrinth is the Minotaur; and, Theseus, you must go thither to seek him.'

'But how shall I ever find him,' asked Theseus, 'if the labyrinth so bewilders me as you say it will?'

Just as he spoke they heard a rough and very disagreeable roar, which greatly resembled the lowing of a fierce bull, but yet had some sort of sound like the human voice. Theseus even fancied a rude articulation in it, as if the creature that uttered it were trying to

shape his hoarse breath into words. It was at some distance, however, and he really could not tell whether it
sounded most like a bull's roar or a man's harsh voice.

'That is the Minotaur's noise,' whispered Ariadne,
closely grasping the hand of Theseus, and pressing one
of her own hands to her heart, which was all in a tremble. 'You must follow that sound through the windings
of the labyrinth, and, by and by, you will find him.
Stay! take the end of this silken string; I will hold the
other end; and then, if you win the victory, it will lead
you again to this spot. Farewell, brave Theseus.'

So the young man took the end of the silken string in
his left hand, and his gold-hilted sword, ready drawn
from its scabbard, in the other, and trod boldly into the
inscrutable labyrinth. How this labyrinth was built is
more than I can tell you, but so cunningly contrived a
mizmaze was never seen in the world before nor since.
There can be nothing else so intricate, unless it were
the brain of a man like Daedalus, who planned it, or
the heart of any ordinary man; which last, to be sure, is
ten times as great a mystery as the labyrinth of Crete.
Theseus had not taken five steps before he lost sight of
Ariadne; and in five more his head was growing dizzy.
But still he went on, now creeping through a low arch,
now ascending a flight of steps, now in one crooked
passage, and now in another, with here a door opening
before him, and there one banging behind, until it
really seemed as if the walls spun round, and whirled
him round along with them. And all the while, through
these hollow avenues, now nearer, now farther off
again, resounded the cry of the Minotaur; and the

sound was so fierce, so cruel, so ugly, so like a bull's roar, and withal so like a human voice, and yet like neither of them, that the brave heart of Theseus grew sterner and angrier at every step; for he felt it an insult to the moon and sky, and to our affectionate and simple Mother Earth, that such a monster should have the audacity to exist.

As he passed onward, the clouds gathered over the moon and the labyrinth grew so dusky that Theseus could no longer discern the bewilderment through which he was passing. He would have felt quite lost, and utterly hopeless of ever again walking in a straight path, if, every little while, he had not been conscious of a gentle twitch at the silken cord. Then he knew that the tender-hearted Ariadne was still holding the other end, and that she was fearing for him, and hoping for him, and giving him just as much of her sympathy as if she were close by his side. Oh, indeed, I can assure you, there was a vast deal of human sympathy running along that slender thread of silk. But still he followed the dreadful roar of the Minotaur, which now grew louder and louder, and finally so very loud that Theseus fully expected to come close upon him at every new zigzag and wriggle of the path. And at last, in an open space at the very centre of the labyrinth, he did discern the hideous creature.

Sure enough, what an ugly monster it was! Only his horned head belonged to a bull; and yet, somehow or other, he looked like a bull all over, preposterously waddling on his hind legs; or, if you happened to view him in another way, he seemed wholly a man, and all the more monstrous for being so. And there he was, the wretched thing, with no society, no companion, no kind of a mate, living only to do mischief, and incapable of knowing what affection means. Theseus hated him, and shuddered at him, and yet could not but be sensible of some sort of pity; and all the more, the uglier and more detestable the creature was. For he kept striding to and fro in a solitary frenzy of rage, continually emitting a hoarse roar, which was oddly mixed up with half-shaped words; and, after listening awhile, Theseus understood that the Minotaur was saying to himself how miserable he was, and how hungry and how he hated everybody, and how he longed to eat up the human race alive.

Ah, the bull-headed villain! And oh, my good little people, you will perhaps see, one of these days, as I do now, that every human being who suffers anything evil to get into his nature, or to remain there, is a kind of Minotaur, an enemy of his fellow-creatures and separated from all good companionship, as this poor monster was.

Was Theseus afraid? By no means, my dear auditors. What! a hero like Theseus afraid! Not even had the Minotaur had twenty heads instead of one. Bold as he was, however, I rather fancy that it strengthened his valiant heart, just at this crisis, to feel a tremulous twitch at the silken cord, which he was still holding in his left hand. It was as if Ariadne were giving him all her might and courage; and, much as he already had, and little as she had to give, it made his own seem twice as much. And to confess the honest truth, he needed the whole; for now the Minotaur, turning suddenly about, caught sight of Theseus, and instantly lowered his horribly sharp horns, exactly as a mad bull does when he means to rush against an enemy. At the same time he belched forth a tremendous roar, in which there was something like the words of human language, but all disjointed and shaken to pieces by passing through the gullet of a miserably enraged brute.

Theseus could only guess what the creature intended to say, and that rather by his gestures than his words; for the Minotaur's horns were sharper than his wits, and of a great deal more service to him than his tongue. But probably this was the sense of what he uttered:

'Ah, wretch of a human being! I'll stick my horns through you, and toss you fifty feet high, and eat you up the moment you come down.'

'Come on then, and try it!' was all that Theseus deigned to reply; for he was far too magnanimous to assault his enemy with insolent language.

Without more words on either side, there ensued the most awful fight between Theseus and the Minotaur that ever happened beneath the sun or moon. I really know not how it might have turned out if the monster, in his first headlong rush against Theseus, had not missed him, by a hair's-breadth, and broken one of his horns short off against the stone wall. On this mishap, he bellowed so intolerably that a part of the labyrinth tumbled down, and all the inhabitants of Crete mistook the noise for an uncommonly heavy thunder-storm. Smarting with the pain, he galloped around the open space in so ridiculous a way that Theseus laughed at it long afterwards, though not precisely at the moment. After this the two antagonists stood valiantly up to one another, and fought sword to horn for a long while. At last the Minotaur made a run at Theseus, grazed his left side with his horn, and flung him down; and, thinking that he had stabbed him to the heart, he cut a great caper in the air, opened his bull mouth from ear to ear, and prepared to snap his head off. But Theseus by this time had leaped up, and caught the monster off

his guard. Fetching a sword stroke at him with all his force, he hit him fair upon the neck, and made his bull head skip six yards from his human body, which fell down flat upon the ground.

So now the battle was ended. Immediately the moon shone out as brightly as if all the troubles of the world, and all the wickedness and the ugliness that infest human life, were past and gone for ever. And Theseus, as he leaned on his sword, taking breath, felt another twitch of the silken cord; for all through the terrible encounter he had held it fast in his left hand. Eager to let Ariadne know of his success, he followed the guidance of the thread, and soon found himself at the entrance of the labyrinth.

'Thou hast slain the monster,' cried Ariadne, clasping her hands.

'Thanks to thee, dear Ariadne,' answered Theseus, 'I return victorious.'

'Then,' said Ariadne, 'we must quickly summon thy friends, and get them and thyself on board the vessel before dawn. If morning finds thee here, my father will avenge the Minotaur.'

To make my story short, the poor captives were awakened, and, hardly knowing whether it was not a joyful dream, were told what Theseus had done, and that they must set sail for Athens before daybreak. Hastening down to the vessel, they all clambered on board, except Prince Theseus, who lingered behind them on the strand, holding Ariadne's hand clasped in his own.

'Dear maiden,' said he, 'thou wilt surely go with us.

Thou art too gentle and sweet a child for such an iron-hearted father as King Minos. He cares no more for thee than a granite rock cares for the little flower that grows in one of its crevices. But my father, King Aegeus, and my dear mother, Aethra, and all the fathers and mothers in Athens, and all the sons and daughters too, will love and honour thee as their benefactress. Come with us, then; for King Minos will be very angry when he knows what thou hast done.'

Now, some low-minded people, who pretend to tell the story of Theseus and Ariadne, have the face to say that this royal and honourable maiden did really flee away under cover of the night, with the young stranger whose life she had preserved. They say, too, that Prince Theseus (who would have died sooner than wrong the meanest creature in the world) ungratefully deserted Ariadne on a solitary island, where the vessel touched on its voyage to Athens. But had the noble Theseus heard these falsehoods, he would have served their slanderous authors as he served the Minotaur! Here is what Ariadne answered, when the brave Prince of Athens besought her to accompany him:

'No, Theseus,' the maiden said, pressing his hand, and then drawing back a step or two, 'I cannot go with you. My father is old, and has nobody but myself to love him. Hard as you think his heart is, it would break to lose me. At first, King Minos will be angry; but he will soon forgive his only child; and, by and by, he will rejoice, I know, that no more youths and maidens must come from Athens to be devoured by the Mino-taur. I have saved you, Theseus, as much for my father's sake as for your own. Farewell! Heaven bless you!'

All this was so true, and so maiden-like, and was spoken with so sweet a dignity, that Theseus would have blushed to urge her any longer. Nothing remained for him, therefore, but to bid Ariadne an affectionate farewell, and go on board the vessel, and set sail.

In a few moments the white foam was boiling up before their prow, as Prince Theseus and his companions sailed out of the harbour, with a whistling breeze behind them. Talus, the brazen giant, on his never-ceasing sentinel's march, happened to be approaching that part of the coast; and they saw him, by the glimmering of the moonbeams on his polished surface, while he was yet a great way off. As the figure moved like a clockwork, however, and could neither hasten his enormous strides nor retard them, he arrived at the port when they were just beyond the reach of his club. Nevertheless, straddling from headland to headland, as his custom was, Talus attempted to strike a blow at the vessel, and, overreaching himself, tumbled at full length into the sea, which splashed high over his gigantic shape, as when an iceberg turns a somersault. There he lies yet; and whoever desires to enrich himself by means of brass had better go thither with a diving-bell, and fish up Talus.

On the homeward voyage the fourteen youths and damsels were in excellent spirits, as you will easily suppose. They spent most of their time in dancing, unless when the side-long breeze made the deck slope too much. In due season they came within sight of the coast of Attica, which was their native country. But here, I am grieved to tell you, happened a sad misfortune.

You will remember (what Theseus unfortunately forgot) that his father, King Aegeus, had enjoined upon him to hoist sunshiny sails, instead of black ones, in case he should overcome the Minotaur, and return victorious. In the joy of their success, however, and amidst the sports, dancing, and other merriment with which these young folks wore away the time, they never once thought whether their sails were black, white or rainbow-coloured, and, indeed, left it entirely to the mariners whether they had any sails at all. Thus the vessel returned, like a raven, with the same sable wings that had wafted her away. But poor King Aegeus, day after day, infirm as he was, had clambered to the summit of a cliff that overhung the sea, and there sat watching for Prince Theseus, homeward bound; and no sooner did he behold the fatal blackness of the sails than he concluded that his dear son, whom he loved so much, and felt so proud of, had been eaten by the Minotaur. He could not bear the thought of living any longer; so, first flinging his crown and sceptre into the sea (useless baubles that they were to him now!) King Aegeus merely stooped forward and fell headlong over the cliff, and was drowned, poor soul, in the waves that foamed at its base!

This was melancholy news for Prince Theseus, who, when he stepped ashore, found himself king of all the country, whether he would or no; and such a turn of fortune was enough to make any young man feel much out of spirits. However, he sent for his dear mother to Athens, and, by taking her advice in matters of state, became a very excellent monarch, and was greatly beloved by his people.

Jean Labadie's Big Black Dog

Once in another time, Jean Labadie was the most popular storyteller in the parish. He acted out every story so that it would seem more real.

When he told about the great falls of Niagara, he made a booming noise deep in his throat and whirled his fists around each other. Then each listener could plainly hear the falls and see the white water churning and splashing as if it were about to pour down on his own head. But Jean Labadie had to stop telling his stories about the *loup-garou*, that demon who takes the shape of a terrible animal and pounces upon those foolish people who go out alone at night. Every time the storyteller dropped down on all fours, rolled his eyes, snorted, and clawed at the floor, his listeners ran away from him in terror.

It was only on the long winter evenings that Jean had time to tell these tales. All the rest of the year, he worked hard with his cows and his pigs and his chickens.

One day Jean Labadie noticed that his flock of chickens was getting smaller and smaller. He began to suspect that his neighbour, André Drouillard, was stealing them. Yet he never could catch André in the act.

For three nights running, Jean took his gun down from the wall and slept in the henhouse with his chickens. But the only thing that happened was that his hens were disturbed by having their feeder roost with them, and they stopped laying well. So Jean sighed and put his gun back and climbed into his own bed again.

One afternoon when Jean went to help his neighbour mow the weeds around his barn, he found a bunch of grey chicken feathers near the fence. Now he was sure that André was taking his chickens, for all of his neighbour's chickens were scrawny white things.

He did not know how to broach the matter to André without making an enemy of him. And when one lives in the country and needs help with many tasks, it is a great mistake to make an enemy of a close neighbour. Jean studied the matter as his scythe went swish, swish through the tall weeds. At last he thought of a way out.

'Have you seen my big black dog, André?' he asked his neighbour.

'What big black dog?' asked André. 'I didn't know you had a dog.'

'I just got him from the Indians,' said Jean. 'Someone has been stealing my chickens so I got myself a dog to protect them. He is a very fierce dog, bigger than a wolf and twice as wild.'

Jean took one hand off the scythe and pointed to the ridge behind the barn.

'There he goes now,' he cried, 'with his big red tongue hanging out of his mouth. See him!'

André looked but could see nothing.

'Surely you must see him. He runs along so fast. He lifts one paw this way and another paw that way.'

As Jean said this, he dropped the scythe and lifted first one hand in its black glove and then the other.

André looked at the black gloves going up and down like the paws of a big black dog. Then he looked toward the ridge. He grew excited.

'Yes, yes,' he cried. 'I do see him now. He is running along the fence. He lifts one paw this way and another paw that way, just like you say.'

Jean was pleased that he was such a good actor he could make André see a dog that didn't exist at all.

'Now that you have seen him,' he said, 'you will know him if you should meet. Give him a wide path and don't do anything that will make him suspicious. He is a very fierce watchdog.'

André promised to stay a safe distance from the big black dog.

Jean Labadie was proud of himself over the success of his trick. No more chickens disappeared. It seemed that his problem was solved.

Then one day André greeted him with, 'I saw your big black dog in the road today. He was running along lifting one paw this way and another paw that way. I got out of his way, you can bet my life!'

Jean Labadie was pleased and annoyed at the same time. Pleased that André believed so completely in the big black dog that he actually could see him. He was also annoyed because the big black dog had been running down the road when he should have been on the farm.

Another day André leaned over the fence.

'Good day, Jean Labadie,' he said. 'I saw your big black dog on the other side of the village. He was jumping over fences and bushes. Isn't it a bad thing for him to wander so far away? Someone might take him for the *loup-garou*.'

Jean Labadie was disgusted with his neighbour's good imagination.

'André,' he asked, 'how can my dog be on the other side of the village when he is right here at home? See him walking through the yard, lifting one paw this way and another paw that way?'

André looked in Jean's yard with surprise.

'And so he is,' he agreed. 'My faith, what a one he is! He must run like lightning to get home so fast. Perhaps you should chain him up. Someone will surely mistake such a fast dog for the *loup-garou*.'

Jean shrugged hopelessly.

'All right,' he said. 'Perhaps you are right. I will chain him near the henhouse.'

'They will be very happy to hear that in the village,' said André. 'Everyone is afraid of him. I have told them all about him, how big and fierce he is, how his long red tongue hangs out of his mouth and how he lifts one paw this way and another paw that way.'

Jean was angry.

'I would thank you to leave my dog alone, André Drouillard,' he said stiffly.

'Oh, ho, and that I do!' retorted André. 'But today on the road he growled and snapped at me. I would not be here to tell the story if I hadn't taken to a tall maple tree.'

Jean Labadie pressed his lips together.

'Then I will chain him up this very moment.' He gave a long low whistle. 'Come, fellow! Here, fellow!'

André Drouillard took to his heels.

Of course, this should have ended the matter, and Jean Labadie thought that it had. But one day when he went to the village to buy some nails for his roof, he ran into Madame Villeneuve in a great how-does-it-make of excitement.

'Jean Labadie,' she cried to him, 'you should be ashamed of yourself, letting that fierce dog run loose in the village.'

'But my dog is chained up in the yard at home,' said Jean.

'So André Drouillard told me,' said Madame, 'but he has broken loose. He is running along lifting one paw this way and another paw that way, with the broken chain dragging in the dust. He growled at me and bared his fangs. It's a lucky thing his chain caught on a bush or I would not be talking to you now.'

Jean sighed.

'Perhaps I should get rid of my big black dog,' he said. 'Tomorrow I will take him back to the Indians.'

So next day Jean hitched his horse to the cart and waited until he saw André Drouillard at work in his garden. Then he whistled loudly toward the yard, made a great show of helping his dog climb up between

146

the wheels and drove past André's house with one arm curved out in a bow, as if it were around the dog's neck.

'Au revoir, André!' he called. Then he looked at the empty half of the seat. 'Bark good-bye to André Drouillard, fellow, for you are leaving here forever.'

Jean drove out to the Indian village and spent the day with his friends, eating and talking. It seemed a bad waste of time when there was so much to be done on the farm, but on the other hand, it was worth idling all day in order to end the big black dog matter.

Dusk was falling as he rounded the curve near his home. He saw the shadowy figure of André Drouillard waiting for him near his gate. A feeling of foreboding came over Jean.

'What is it?' he asked his neighbour. 'Do you have some bad news for me?'

'It's about your big black dog,' said André. 'He has come back home. Indeed he beat you by an hour. It was that long ago I saw him running down the road to your house with his big red tongue hanging out of his mouth and lifting one paw this way and another paw that way.'

Jean was filled with rage. For a twist of tobacco, he would have struck André with his horsewhip.

'André Drouillard,' he shouted, 'you are a liar! I just left the big black dog with the Indians. They have tied him up.'

André sneered.

'A liar, am I? We shall see who is the liar. Wait until the others see your big black dog running around again.'

So Jean might as well have accused André of being a chicken thief in the first place, for now they were enemies anyway. And he certainly might as well have stayed home and fixed his roof.

Things turned out as his neighbour had hinted. Madame Villeneuve saw the big black dog running behind her house. Henri Dupuis saw him running around the corner of the store. Delphine Langlois even saw him running through the graveyard among the tombstones. And always as he ran along, he lifted one paw this way and another paw that way.

There came that day when Jean Labadie left his neighbour chopping wood all by himself, because they were no longer friends, and drove into the village to have his black mare shod. While he was sitting in front of the blacksmith shop, André Drouillard came galloping up at a great speed. He could scarcely hold the reins, for one hand was cut and bleeding.

A crowd quickly gathered.

'What is wrong, André Drouillard?' they asked.

'Have you cut yourself?'

'Where is Dr Brisson? Someone fetch Dr Brisson.'

André Drouillard pointed his bleeding hand at Jean Labadie.

'His big black dog bit me,' he accused. 'Without warning, he jumped the fence as soon as Jean drove away and sank his teeth into my hand.'

There was a gasp of horror from every throat. Jean Labadie reddened. He walked over to André and stared at the wound.

'It looks like an axe cut to me,' he said.

Then everyone grew angry at Jean Labadie and his big black dog. They threatened to drive them both out of the parish.

'My friends,' said Jean wearily, 'I think it is time for this matter to be ended. The truth of it is that I have no big black dog. I never had a big black dog. It was all a joke.'

'Aha!' cried André. 'Now he is trying to crawl out of the blame. He says he has no big black dog. Yet I have seen it with my own eyes, running around and lifting one paw this way and another paw that way.'

'I have seen it, too,' cried Madame Villeneuve. 'It ran up and growled at me.'

'And I.'

'And I.'

Jean Labadie bowed his head.

'All right, my friends,' he said. 'There is nothing more I can do about it. I guess that big black dog will eat me out of house and home for the rest of my life.'

'You mean you won't make things right about this hand?' demanded André Drouillard.

'What do you want me to do?' asked Jean.

'I will be laid up for a week at least,' said André Drouillard, 'and right at harvest time. Then, too, there may be a scar. But for two of your plumpest pullets, I am willing to overlook the matter and be friends again.'

'That is fair,' cried Henri Dupuis.

'It is just,' cried the blacksmith.

'A generous proposal,' agreed everyone.

'And now we will return to my farm,' said Jean Labadie, 'and I will give André two of my pullets. But all of you must come. I want witnesses.'

A crowd trooped down the road to watch the transaction. It was almost as large as the one that had attended Tante Odette's skunk party.

After Jean had given his neighbour two of his best pullets, he commanded the crowd, 'Wait!'

He went into the house. When he returned, he was carrying his gun.

'I want witnesses,' explained Jean, 'because I am going to shoot my big black dog. I want everyone to see this happen.'

The crowd murmured and surged. Jean gave a long low whistle toward the henhouse.

'Here comes my big black dog,' he pointed. 'You can see how he runs to me with his big red tongue hanging out and lifting one paw this way and another paw that way.'

Everyone saw the big black dog.

Jean Labadie lifted his gun to his shoulder, pointed it at nothing and pulled the trigger. There was a deafening roar and the gun kicked Jean to the ground. He arose and brushed off his blouse. Madame Villeneuve screamed and Delphine Langlois fainted.

'There,' said Jean, brushing away a tear, 'it is done. That is the end of my big black dog. Isn't that true?'

And everyone agreed that the dog was gone for good.

So remember this, my friends: If you must make up a big black dog, do not allow others to help or you may find that you are no longer the dog's master.

The Night the Bed Fell

I suppose that the high-water mark of my youth in Columbus, Ohio, was the night the bed fell on my father. It makes a better recitation (unless, as some friends of mine have said, one has heard it five or six times) than it does a piece of writing, for it is almost necessary to throw furniture around, shake doors, and bark like a dog, to lend the proper atmosphere and verisimilitude to what is admittedly a somewhat incredible tale. Still, it did take place.

It happened, then, that my father had decided to sleep in the attic one night, to be away where he could think. My mother opposed the notion strongly because, she said, the old wooden bed up there was unsafe: it was wobbly and the heavy headboard would crash down on father's head in case the bed fell, and kill him. There was no dissuading him, however, and at a quarter past ten he closed the attic door behind him and went up the narrow twisting stairs. We later heard ominous creakings as he crawled into bed. Grandfather, who usually slept in the attic bed when he was with us, had disappeared some days before. (On these occasions he was usually gone six or eight days and returned growling and out of temper, with the news that the Federal Union was run by a passel of blockheads and that the Army of the Potomac didn't have any more chance than a fiddler's bitch.)

We had visiting us at this time a nervous first cousin of mine named Briggs Beall, who believed that he was likely to cease breathing when he was asleep. It was his feeling that if he were not awakened every hour during the night, he might die of suffocation. He had been accustomed to setting an alarm clock to ring at intervals until morning, but I persuaded him to abandon this. He slept in my room and I told him that I was such a light sleeper that if anybody quit breathing in the same room with me, I would wake instantly. He tested me the first night – which I had suspected he would – by holding his breath after my regular breathing had convinced him I was asleep. I was not asleep, however, and called to him. This seemed to allay his fears a little, but he took the precaution of putting a glass of spirits of camphor on a little table at the head of his bed. In case I didn't arouse him until he was almost gone, he said, he would sniff the camphor, a powerful reviver. Briggs was not the only member of his family who had his crotchets. Old Aunt Melissa Beall (who could whistle like a man, with two fingers in her mouth) suffered under the premonition that she was destined to die on South High Street, because she had been born on South High Street and married on South High Street. Then there was Aunt Sarah Shoaf, who never went to bed at night without the fear that a burglar was going to get in and blow chloroform under her door through a tube. To avert this calamity – for she was in greater dread of anaesthetics than of losing her household goods – she always piled her money, silverware, and other valuables in a neat stack just outside her bedroom, with a note reading: 'This is all I have. Please take it and do not use your chloroform, as this is all I have.' Aunt Gracie Shoaf also had a burglar phobia, but she met it with more fortitude. She was confident that burglars had been getting into her house every night for forty years. The fact that she never missed anything was to her no proof to the contrary. She always claimed that she scared them off before they could take anything, by throwing shoes down the hallway. When she went to bed she piled, where she could get at them handily, all the shoes there were about her house. Five minutes after she had turned off the light, she would sit up in bed and say 'Hark!' Her husband, who had learned to ignore the whole situation as long ago as 1903, would either be sound asleep or pretend to be sound asleep. In either case he would not respond to her tugging and pulling, so that presently she would arise, tiptoe to the door, open it slightly and heave a shoe down the hall in one direction, and its mate down the hall in the other direction. Some nights she threw them all, some nights only a couple of pair.

But I am straying from the remarkable incidents that took place during the night that the bed fell on father. By midnight we were all in bed. The layout of the rooms and the disposition of their occupants is important to an understanding of what later occurred. In the front room upstairs (just under father's attic bedroom) were my mother and my brother Herman, who sometimes sang in his sleep, usually 'Marching Through Georgia' or 'Onward Christian Soldiers'. Briggs Beall and myself were in a room adjoining this one. My brother Roy was in a room across the hall from ours. Our dog, Rex, slept in the hall.

My bed was an army cot, one of those affairs which are made wide enough to sleep on comfortably only by putting up, flat with the middle section, the two sides which ordinarily hang down like the sideboards of a drop-leaf table. When these sides are up, it is perilous to roll too far towards the edge, for then the cot is likely to tip completely over, bringing the whole bed down on top of one, with a tremendous banging crash. This, in fact, is precisely what happened, about two o'clock in the morning. (It was my mother who, in recalling the scene later, first referred to it as 'the night the bed fell on your father'.)

Always a deep sleeper, slow to arouse (I had lied to Briggs), I was at first unconscious of what had happened when the iron cot rolled me onto the floor and toppled over on me. It left me still warmly bundled up and unhurt, for the bed rested above me like a canopy. Hence I did not wake up, only reached the edge of consciousness and went back. The racket, however, instantly awakened my mother, in the next room, who came to the immediate conclusion that her worst dread was realized: the big wooden bed upstairs had fallen on father. She therefore screamed, 'Let's go to your poor father!' It was this shout, rather than the noise of my cot falling, that awakened Herman, in the same room with her. He thought that mother had become, for no apparent reason, hysterical. 'You're all right, Mamma!' he shouted, trying to calm her. They exchanged shout for shout for perhaps ten seconds. 'Let's go to your poor father!' and 'You're all right!' That woke up Briggs. By this time I was conscious of what was going on, in a vague way, but did not yet realize that I was under my bed instead of on it. Briggs, awakening in the midst of loud shouts of fear and apprehension, came to the quick conclusion that he was suffocating and that we were all trying to 'bring him out'. With a low moan, he grasped the glass of camphor at the head of his bed and instead of sniffing it poured it over himself. The room reeked of camphor. 'Ugf, ahfg,' choked Briggs, like a drowning man, for he had almost succeeded in stopping his breath under the deluge of pungent spirits. He leapt out of bed and groped toward the open window, but he came up against one that was closed. With his hand, he beat out the glass, and I could hear it crash and tinkle on the alleyway below. It was at this juncture that I, in trying to get up, had the uncanny sensation of feeling my bed above me! Foggy with sleep, I now suspected, in my turn, that the whole uproar was being made in a frantic endeavour to extricate me from what must be an unheard-of and perilous situation. 'Get me out of this!' I bawled. 'Get me out!' I think I had the nightmarish belief that I was entombed in a mine. 'Gugh,' gasped Briggs, floundering in his camphor.

By this time my mother, still shouting, pursued by Herman, still shouting, was trying to open the door to the attic, in order to go up and get my father's body out of the wreckage. The door was stuck, however, and wouldn't yield. Her frantic pulls on it only added to the general banging and confusion. Roy and the dog were now up, the one shouting questions, the other barking.

Father, farthest away and soundest sleeper of all, had by this time been awakened by the battering on the attic door. He decided that the house was on fire. 'I'm coming, I'm coming!' he wailed in a slow, sleepy voice – it took him many minutes to regain full consciousness. My mother, still believing he was caught under the bed, detected in his 'I'm coming!' the

mournful, resigned note of one who is preparing to meet his Maker. 'He's dying!' she shouted.

'I'm all right!' Briggs yelled to reassure her. 'I'm all right!' He still believed that it was his own closeness to death that was worrying mother. I found at last the light switch in my room, unlocked the door, and Briggs and I joined the others at the attic door. The dog, who never did like Briggs, jumped for him – assuming that he was the culprit in whatever was going on – and Roy had to throw Rex and hold him. We could hear father crawling out of bed upstairs. Roy pulled the attic door open, with a mighty jerk, and father came down the stairs, sleepy and irritable but safe and sound. My mother began to weep when she saw him. Rex began to howl. 'What in the name of God is going on here?' asked father.

The situation was finally put together like a gigantic jigsaw puzzle. Father caught a cold from prowling around in his bare feet but there were no other bad results. 'I'm glad,' said mother, who always looked on the bright side of things, 'that your grandfather wasn't here.'

STEPHEN CORRIN

Finn Mac Coole

Hundreds of years ago, in the province of Munster in southern Ireland, Coole, Lord of the Clan Beeskna and Captain of the Fenians of Erin, fought a bloody battle at Cnucha against Aed Mac Morna, Lord of the Clan Morna. During the fighting Aed Mac Morna was wounded in the eye, for which reason he was afterwards called Goll (one-eyed) Mac Morna. Goll, in his fury, killed Coole and stole from his belt a mysterious blue-red bag, which was in fact the Treasure Bag of the Fenians. From that moment on there raged a terrible feud between Clan Beeskna and Clan Morna. The warriors of Clan Beeskna, defeated in battle, sought refuge in the Connacht hills.

Goll Mac Morna then claimed the leadership of all the Fenians. He gave the Treasure Bag to Lia of Luachair, because it was Lia, a Connacht chieftain, who had inflicted the first wound on Coole at the battle of Cnucha.

In the meantime, Coole's wife, Muirna of the White Neck, fled into hiding with some faithful women of her household. She was pregnant, but she knew that no offspring of hers would be safe from the vengeance of Goll Mac Morna and his followers. So when her child was born she gave him into the care of her two most loyal servants and before her death she asked them to bring him up in secret until he grew to manhood, by which time he would be able to challenge Goll Mac Morna for the leadership of the Fenians. She had named him Demna and as he grew up the two women trained him to hunt and to fish and to throw the spear and to learn the ways of the animals that lived in the wilds. He soon became so skilled a hunter that with one single throw of the spear he could bring down a bird in flight, and so swiftly could he run that he could overtake deer without the aid of hounds. He would wander far and wide through the mountains and bogs, so that soon all the sights and sounds of nature were familiar to him.

One day during his wanderings, Demna happened to pass near the home of a famous chieftain on the plain of Liffey, where he saw some boys of about his own age playing hurling. They invited Demna to join in, gave him a hurley stick and explained the rules of the game. In less than no time Demna was playing better than any of them, running faster and capturing the ball from the nimblest. The boys were so much impressed that they set a quarter of all their players against him alone, but Demna won all the same. The next day they played half their number against him, but he was still the victor. The following day their entire number tried their luck against him, but he won those games too. The boys were amazed at his astonishing skill and swiftness and told their chieftain about this remarkable youth. They described him as being very tall and with hair as bright as barley glistening in the sun at harvest time.

'Ah!' exclaimed the chieftain. 'If his hair is truly as fair as you say, there can be only one name for him, and that is Finn.' And from that day onward, Demna was known as Finn (meaning fair or white).

Finn's fame spread like wild-fire throughout the country and soon reached the ears of Goll Mac Morna. 'This clever boy,' he thought, 'sounds perilously like the son of my old rival Coole.' And he recalled how Muirna of the White Neck had gone into hiding and the rumours of the birth of her son as she fled south with the faithful women of her household. Finn must be now about fifteen, old enough to threaten Goll's leadership of the Fenians. Goll lost no time in gathering around him the great Fenian warriors of Connacht and ordering them to hunt down the son of Coole and to bring him back, dead or alive.

But one of the women who had looked after Finn since his birth heard of these hunters and told him about them. 'You must flee from this place as fast as you can,' she warned. 'Goll Mac Morna's men are searching for you. Goll knows that it is you, Finn, son of Coole, who are the rightful Captain of the Fenians and he fears that one day you will conquer him and claim what is yours by right.' So Finn Mac Coole thanked the loyal woman and, gathering up his hunting gear, he set off to roam the country, seeking out other chieftains to serve.

When he was with the King of Kerry, he displayed such rare skill, both with every weapon and in chess, that the King asked where he hailed from.

'My people are peasants from the district of Tara,'

replied Finn vaguely. But the King did not believe him.

'You are no peasant's son,' he said. 'You must indeed be that child whom Muirna of the White Neck gave birth to when she was fleeing from the followers of Goll Mac Morna. That man now seeks to kill you. You can stay here no longer, for I would be no match for Goll Mac Morna.'

This happened again and again. Wherever Finn went, his unbelievable skill and his princely bearing gave him away, and so nobody dared grant him refuge for fear of the vengeance of Goll Mac Morna.

The only thing left to Finn was to gather round himself a band of youths who had the same courage, daring and skill in war as he had himself. This he did, and after many months he set forth for Connacht, where the surviving followers of his father Coole had been hiding since their defeat at Cnucha. One day he came upon a woman wailing and lamenting over the body of a young man.

'What evil men were the cause of this?' asked Finn.

The woman's eyes were blood-red with tears as she replied, 'Lia of Luachair and his band have slain my only son Glonda, who lies dead before you. If you are the warrior you seem to be, you have the duty to avenge his death.'

Finn started at the mention of that name, for he knew that it was Lia of Luachair who had wounded his father at the battle of Cnucha. At once he sought him out and slew him with his own hands in the presence of his followers. Then he noticed a strange-looking bag

fastened to the dead man's belt. Opening it, he found
inside a dark-blue steel spearhead, a helmet, a bronze-
studded shield and a boar-skin belt. He tied the bag to
his own belt and continued his way with his companions. Westward they went, beyond the River Shan-
non and deep into the forest of Connacht, and
suddenly, in a glade, they came upon a rough-look-
ing hut made of plaited branches. When they called,
out came several extremely thin, gaunt, bearded old
men, scantily clothed in crude animal skins and carrying
a few rusty weapons. Yet there was something noble
and dignified about them that made Finn cry out, 'Are
you not indeed the men of Clan Beeskna? And if you
are, which among you is Crimnal, brother of Coole?'

One of the men stepped forward. 'I am Crimnal,
brother of Coole,' he said. Then Finn went down on
his knees before the old man and, laying at his feet the
strange bag he had taken from Lia of Luachair's belt,
he said, 'I am Finn, son of Coole.' Crimnal raised him
and looked at the contents of the bag. As he took them
out one by one, his companions seemed to lose their
bent old age and became straight-backed and young,
as did Crimnal himself.

'This is the Treasure Bag of the Fenians, the same
that Goll Mac Morna took from Coole as he lay dead
on the battlefield of Cnucha! Now what has been fore-
told will surely come to pass: Clan Beeskna will once
more rule the Fenians and you, Finn Mac Coole, will
take your rightful place, your father's place, as Lord of
the Fenians.'

Finn then bade farewell to all his friends, leaving the

Treasure Bag with them, and set off to study the ancient wisdom, learning and poetry of his people at the home of a wise man named Finnegas. All this he had to do to be worthy to succeed to his father's place. Finnegas desired above all things to acquire the entire wisdom of the world and to do this he must catch Fintan, the Salmon of Knowledge, which lived in a dark pool of a river nearby. For whoever ate of that Salmon would possess the wisdom of all the ages, because the Salmon itself had fed on the nuts of the great hazel tree which overhung the river.

Finn had not been studying long with Finnegas when the latter at last caught the coveted fish. Finnegas gave the Salmon to Finn to roast and warned him to be careful not to eat or even to taste one single morsel of it.

'Bring it to me as soon as it is well roasted, for I have been waiting these seven weary years to savour its flesh,' said Finnegas solemnly.

After a while Finn brought in the fish and served it to his master. Finnegas was struck by the radiant look that had come over Finn's face.

'Have you eaten any of the Salmon?' he asked him.

'None at all, master,' replied Finn, 'but when I was turning it on the spit, I burned my thumb and licked it to soothe the pain.'

Finnegas fetched a deep sigh. 'Enough,' he said, 'for the juice of the Salmon has passed into you and you have acquired all the knowledge that was in it. I cannot teach you anything more,' and he gave Finn the rest of the fish to eat.

From that day on, whenever Finn wished to have a knowledge of what would happen in the future, he had but to put his burnt thumb to his lips and the knowledge would immediately come to him.

Finn now felt fully prepared and equipped to claim his father's place as head of the Fenians. It was November, the season of the great festival of Samain, and so Finn made his way west and then north on the road to the High King's Hall at Tara. Kings and chieftains from all parts of the land were on their way there to attend the Great Assembly, where all the chiefs of Erin as well as all ordinary men were free to sit at the table in the High King's Hall. Many of the warriors were deadly enemies of one another and so, by the King's decree, all weapons were to be left outside the Hall.

All eyes were upon Finn as he took his seat, for his bright-gold hair and noble bearing immediately attracted attention. The High King, Con of the Hundred Battles, told the wine-server to offer a goblet of wine to the handsome stranger and to ask his name. Finn rose to his feet and in a clear voice said, 'I am Finn, son of Coole, who, at the time of his death, was Commander of the Fenians of Erin. I have now come, O King, to offer you the service of my sword, and to act at your behest.' The King replied, 'Your father was indeed a mighty hero, a father to be proud of. I will put my trust in your sword as I did in his.' Then he gave Finn a place near his own seat at the table and solemnly bound him in allegiance to himself.

After feasting at the table had gone on for some time, the King rose and said:

'You all know, my lords and chieftains, that for these past twenty years the city of Tara has been laid waste by the unholy monster, Aillinne of the Flaming Breath, and that his devilish custom is to come here this very night, at Samain time, to burn this city to the ground with his fiery breath. Late at night he comes, and with the sweet and sinister music which he plays on his harp of silver he puts all men into a drowsy stupor, so that it is not possible to slay him in fair combat. As yet no warrior has been bold enough to come forward and try his strength and courage against him. I now call upon each and every one of you to show your daring and fight this evil thing.'

The King waited, but nobody stirred. At last Finn rose from his seat. 'If I can prevail against this monster and keep Tara free from his flames, I will ask no reward, but will you swear a solemn oath to restore me to my rightful heritage?'

'And what heritage is that?' asked the King.

'The Captaincy of the Fenians of Erin,' replied Finn.

'I give you my royal pledge that that will be so and that Goll Mac Morna shall cede that Captaincy to you if you can overcome Aillinne of the Flaming Breath.'

At this everyone stared at Goll Mac Morna, but he looked straight ahead of him, expressionless, and said not a word.

Finn then rose, bowed to the King and left the Hall, picking up the spear he had put down at the entrance. But he did not leave alone. He was followed by an old man named Fiacha, whose life Coole had once saved.

Finn went out on to the ramparts and began to walk round to start his lonely vigil. Deep in thought, he did not notice Fiacha, who suddenly spoke out:

'Finn Mac Coole,' he said, 'long ago your noble father saved my life. I now hand you this enchanted spear in repayment for the debt I owe him. This spear will do much more than your own, for it was forged by Len, swordsmith to the gods. As soon as you hear the bewitching sounds from the monster's silver harp, place the spear-blade to your brow and all drowsiness will leave you.'

Finn accepted the spear gratefully and began once more to pace the ramparts. It was not long before the strains of Aillinne's music reached his ears. Louder and more hauntingly melodious they became and Finn listened enraptured, oblivious of everything save the enchanting sounds. An overwhelming feeling of sleepiness came over him and his eyelids were leaden, but with a superhuman effort he raised Fiacha's spear and pressed the cold blue steel to his forehead. One powerful single note came from the weapon, which seemed to drive away the magic sounds and take their place. Then in the distance he espied the ghost-like form of Aillinne of the Flaming Breath approaching. As he came nearer and nearer, a long tongue of flame preceded him. But Finn, quicker than lightning, tore off his mantle and flung it over the flame, beating it to the ground. Aillinne gave an eerie wail, twisted round and turned back. Finn leaped after him and cast his spear at the monster, piercing his body right through. Aillinne of the Flaming Breath lay dead in all his hideous ugliness, and Finn cut off his head with his sword, impaled it on his spear, and set it up on the walls of Tara so that all might witness it.

By next morning everyone knew that the city was free for ever more from the monster's depredations. The King himself appeared on the ramparts and standing beside Finn proclaimed:

'I now honour my pledged word of yesternight and solemnly bestow the Captaincy of the Fenians on this heroic young warrior. He has vanquished the Evil Thing and saved us from its ravagings.' And to Goll Mac Morna the King said, 'Will you now lay your hand on Finn's or will you leave us to enter the service of others?' Goll replied, 'I will lay my hand on Finn's.' Then in the presence of the King and the Fenians he swore an oath of allegiance to Finn Mac Coole, and all the other warriors followed suit and vowed their loyalty to their new Captain.

And thus it came to pass that Finn Mac Coole became Head of the Fenians.

Finn now rejoined his old companions. All his men were tried and trusted warriors, for it was no easy task to become a member of that proud brotherhood. Not only did a man have to be brave and skilful with every manner of weapon but he had to be able to stand in a sedgy field with nothing to defend himself but a shield and hazel stick the length of his arm. Nine men, all at the same time, threw javelins at him and the aspiring warrior had to ward them off and escape unscathed. Another test was to be pursued through the woods by a number of soldiers, with the start of only the girth of a tree-trunk. If he was overtaken or wounded, if one single strand of his plaited hair became undone, or even if a withered branch of a tree crackled underfoot as he ran, he had failed. Another test was to leap over a tree as high as his forehead and stoop under a fallen tree no higher than his knee, and while still running his fastest he had to draw a thorn from his foot. As far as learning was concerned, any would-be Fenian had to memorize all the twelve books of ancient poetry and most of the old stories as well. Once he had passed these tests he was admitted and was bound by four pledges: not to accept a dowry in marriage, not to capture cattle by force of arms, never to refuse to go to the help of anyone, and never to surrender in combat to fewer than nine opponents.

One day Finn Mac Coole was out hunting with his companions when one of them espied a boat pulling in towards the shore. They waited till the boat had grounded on the shingle. A tall, handsome man sprang from the boat and came hurrying towards them.

'You are the son of Coole, Lord of all the Fenians, are you not?' he asked Finn.

'Yes,' was the reply. 'What brings you here?'

'I have come to ask you to save my child. I have already lost two and I fear I may lose the next. You are the only man who could possibly save him.'

'And what if I refuse to help you?' asked Finn.

'Then I will lay a spell on you so that you will not eat, drink or sleep unless you follow me first.' And with these words the handsome stranger strode back to his boat and his crew rapidly rowed away from the shore. Finn went and told his companions what the stranger had said to him and continued, 'Since I am pledged never to withhold help from anyone in need and am now placed under a spell not to eat, drink or sleep, I have no choice but to follow the man.' His companions wanted to accompany him, but he refused and went down to the shore alone.

He had not gone very far among the rocks and shingle when he was accosted by seven men, who greeted him and offered him their services. Each of them was capable of accomplishing a superhuman deed. One could fell an alder tree in three strokes, saw it into planks and build a ship. Another was a tracker and could hunt down wild birds over land and sea in

one day. A third could grip and uproot the mightiest tree.
The fourth could climb to the stars on a stairway as light
as gossamer. The fifth was such a skilful thief, he could
steal a heron's egg from her nest under the very eyes of
the mother bird. The sixth could hear a whisper from
the other end of the world. And the seventh was such a
perfect marksman that he could shoot an arrow into an
egg that had been shot into the skies with all the force
with which the strongest bowman could send his arrow.
Finn was glad to accept such valuable services, so the
Shipwright built a ship on the spot and they immediately set sail in pursuit of the strange man.

Before long they came to a beach where the man's
boat lay. They leaped ashore and ran towards a great

house in the glen overlooking the beach. They saw the stranger coming out to meet them, his arms outstretched in welcome, and when he was near enough he embraced them warmly.

'I am indeed happy that you decided to come to my aid,' he said. He gave them food and drink in plenty and then led them to a quiet place where they could rest. And afterwards he told them his story.

'Six years ago my wife bore me a son, but on the very night that he was born a great hand came down the chimney and took the child away. Three years later the same thing happened when she bore her second son. Tonight my wife is going to give birth to her third child. You, Finn Mac Coole, are the only man, I am told, who can save this new-born infant.'

'Rest assured,' said Finn, 'I myself will keep watch for this dread menace.' And he told his men to stretch themselves out full length on the floor. Just before midnight the baby was born and the terrible hand came down the chimney. Finn called upon the man who could uproot the mightiest tree-trunk and told him to grip the hand. Then there took place the most tremendous tug-of-war between the hand and the man. One moment the man was pulled half-way up the chimney and the next the hand was pulled down as far as the armpit, and this went on for several hours. At last, with one mighty wrench, the hand was pulled clean out of its shoulder socket. But, alas, another giant hand then came down the chimney and stole the baby away.

Finn was not daunted. 'Before dawn my men and I will set out to seek this hand, and if we do not bring your child back safely, may none of us ever see our own home again.'

At sunrise they set off, the Tracker instructing Finn where to steer the ship. At sunset they landed on an island rock, on top of which was a tower. The Climber was on top of it in a flash and down again just as quickly.

'What did you see up there?' asked Finn.

'Through a hole in the roof I saw a giant lying on a bed with a silken coverlet over him and a satin sheet under him. There was a baby asleep on the palm of his hand and two boys were playing with a silver ball near the bed. And by the hearth was a deer-hound suckling her two pups.'

'Then up you go again,' said Finn, 'but this time you must carry the Thief on your back.' And quick as the wind the two were up top again and down. This time the Thief was carrying the baby, the two boys, and the two pups, as well as the coverlet of silk and the satin undersheet.

They put everything in the boat and sailed away again. All too soon, however, the Listener told Finn that he could hear the giant fuming and raging and telling the deerhound to swim after them. And indeed, there she was, swimming furiously and almost touching their boat.

'Throw down one of her pups to her,' commanded Finn. This they did and the hound picked it up in her teeth and swam back with it. But in next to no time the giant himself was after them, for the hound would not leave her pup to come chasing a second time. Then

Finn put his wisdom-thumb to his lips and learned that the giant was invulnerable except for a tiny mole on the palm of his right hand. Finn told the Marksman about this. 'Just let me catch one glimpse of that mole,' said the Marksman, 'and your giant is a dead man.' By this time the giant had reached the boat's side and put up his right hand to seize the top of the mast. The Marksman sighted the mole and shot an arrow right through it. The giant fell dead into the sea with an enormous splash. Then Finn told the men to turn back to get the second pup from the tower and when this had been achieved they set sail once again for the stranger's house.

'What reward do you ask?' said the stranger to Finn, overjoyed to have this three children safely restored to him.

'I ask only that I may choose one of these two pups,' said Finn. That request the stranger most willingly granted and Finn chose a pup, which he named Bran, whilst the stranger kept the other, which he named Grey Dog. He then bade them farewell and watched as they sailed back to their own land.

Many years later, Finn and his companions were out hunting one day, when they saw a tall youth coming towards them. He approached Finn and told him he had come to seek a master to serve for a year and a day.

'Just such a one as you is what I am needing,' said Finn, 'but what reward will you be asking at the end of that year and a day?'

'Only that you will come with me and feast in the palace of the King of Lochlan,' replied the tall youth. Finn agreed to this and the lad entered his service.

A year and a day passed and the young man asked Finn if he was satisfied with the way he had served him.

'Yes,' replied Finn. 'I am fully satisfied and I shall go with you to the palace of the King of Lochlan,' and he told his men where he was going. 'I do not know when I shall be back, but if I do not return after a year and a day, be sure to sharpen your swords and make ready your bows to avenge me on the shore of Lochlan.'

To his jester, who was sitting weeping by the fireside, Finn said, 'You should not now be sad but giving me good advice and cheer to spur me on my journey.'

'I am not in the mood to be making you cheerful,' replied the jester. 'But I can give you some advice if you are prepared to follow it.'

'And what is that advice?' asked Finn.

'Take the golden chain of your hound, Bran, with you,' was the brief reply.

Finn accepted the advice of his jester and set off on his journey with the tall youth. The latter sped on so swiftly that it was all Finn could do to keep him in sight, but at last they reached the King of Lochlan's palace and Finn, who much to his surprise felt quite exhausted, sat down among the chiefs. But there was no feast awaiting him. On the contrary, the lords in the palace started to dispute about the speediest way of putting him to death, for these men were the Fenians' bitterest foes and Finn had been lured there by the treacherous youth.

'Hang him!' cried one noble. 'Burn him!' shouted another. 'Drown him!' cried a third. 'No! No!' demanded a fourth. 'Let him be killed by the Grey Dog, for no man has returned alive from his lair since we captured him in our raid on the glen: that would be the most humiliating death for the head of the Fenians!' They all agreed to this, and Finn was taken by force far up into the glen where the howling of the Grey Dog could be heard. Then the lords of Lochlan fled in fear, leaving Finn to the mercies of the savage cur. His mouth wide open and his tongue hanging to one side, the Grey Dog came towards him, breathing his flaming breath. Finn knew that he would not be able to bear its heat for long. Now was the time, he thought, to make use of Bran's golden chain. He put his hand into his pocket and when the Grey Dog was almost upon him, he shook the chain. Immediately the Grey Dog came to a halt and wagged his tail. Then he licked Finn's burning wounds from head to foot and healed them. Finn put the chain round the Grey Dog's neck and led him back down the glen.

He was met by an old woman and her husband. 'You must be Finn, Lord of the Fenians,' they said, 'and that must be Bran's golden chain. No other mortal man could lead the Grey Dog like that.' And they invited Finn to stay at their house for a year and a day.

At the end of that time Finn's great army of men came to fetch him, as he had asked them. Their shouts of greeting were heard by the men of Lochlan and the Fenians pursued these men and took vengeance upon them for the way they had treated Finn. As for the Grey Dog, he gave a most friendly greeting to Bran, for they were the two pups Finn had taken from the giant's tower. Finn re-named the Grey Dog Skolaun, and so he now had two faithful hounds to follow always at their master's heels.

Then they all returned to their homes and made a great feast, which lasted for a year and a day.

Another afternoon in high summer, when Finn and his Fenians had been hunting over the length and breadth of their land, they saw coming towards them the ugliest man you could ever imagine, and this man was leading the most unbeautiful horse ever ridden by a hunter. The man was a bow-legged giant with an awkwardly shaped, twisted body, crooked teeth extending well over his lower lip (which was an incredibly fat one) and with arms long enough to touch the ground. He was dragging along behind him an enormous, heavy, cumbersome fork, which furrowed up the earth like a farmer's plough. The giant's horse was as outlandish-looking as his master, covered all over with black, dirty hair. All his skinny ribs showed through his worn, scarred hide, and round his neck, which was far too long even for his enormous body, was a halter which the giant was pulling with all his might. Whenever the horse showed an inclination to pause, the giant would beat him mercilessly with the iron fork. The giant at length reached the crest of the hill where

Finn and his men were standing. Without waiting to be asked, he bawled out: 'I have never known who my father and mother were, but people call me the Giolla Dacker. I sell my services to anyone willing to feed and pay me for them. I have heard of you, Finn Mac Coole, and am willing to serve you for one year.'

'And what wages are you asking?' said Finn.

'As for that, I will decide when the year is up,' the giant shouted back. 'And I must also warn you that I am the laziest servant that ever was and that I grumble about anything and everything, even when I am given the simplest task.'

Finn listened with amusement and said, 'I have always given work to those who seek it and I will offer you some now, despite your own bad recommendation.'

Without a word of thanks the giant removed the halter from his horse's neck, at which the strange animal began running about wildly in all directions, furiously shaking his long neck and kicking out at anyone within reach. The Fenians ran away in alarm and shouted to the Giolla Dacker to catch hold of the beast before he did any harm. The giant merely tossed the halter to them, saying, 'You had better do your own dirty work.' One of the men, Conan by name, snatched up the halter and managed to fling it round the long neck, but when he tried to drag the beast towards him, the horse became as immovable as a rock. Conan stood there, purple with rage and humiliation, while his companions looked on shaking with laughter at the ridiculous spectacle. Then the heaviest of the

Fenians, Coil Crodag, sprang on to the horse's back, kicked him in the ribs for all he was worth and banged him with the flat of his sword, but all to no avail. Several more men mounted behind Coil but still the animal refused to budge a single inch.

Then the Giolla Dacker put on a great show of indignation. 'Why do you do nothing to stop your men making mock of my steed?' he cried to Finn. 'I won't put up with this from you or from anybody! Give me my wages and let me get away from this vile place!'

'Oh no,' replied Finn, 'not one minute before you have completed your year's service, according to our bargain.'

'In that case I will not wait for your money. I'll be off straight away and offer my services to another,' bawled the giant, and off he lumbered. His horse began slowly trotting after him in the most ungainly fashion, with Finn's men still on his back. Then quite unexpectedly the Giolla Dacker put on a tremendous burst of speed and the horse galloped after him at such a rate that the unwilling riders were unable to dismount and had to cling on for dear life.

The rest of the men now saw that this was no laughing matter and started off in hot pursuit down to the coast, only to see the Giolla Dacker and his mount dash right out into the sea. The swiftest of the Fenians, Ligan Lumina, who could also jump further than any other man, gave one mighty leap and caught the horse by the tail, only to be towed helplessly along behind.

Finn, at the water's edge, decided it was no use wasting time just standing there, equally helpless. With fifteen of his bravest followers, including his old enemy, Goll Mac Morna, and young Diarmuid O'Dyna, he headed south to Ben Eader, where a ship was always ready in case of need.

After sailing for many days, they espied an island rising up heavenwards straight out of the sea, and they sailed round and round it, looking for a way to reach its top. Now the only man who could possibly do this was young Diarmuid O'Dyna, who had been taught the secret ways of enchanted peoples by his divine foster-father, Aengus Mac Oc. So Diarmuid, his two long spears in either hand, gave one great leap and landed on a narrow ledge of the island's summit. In front of him lay vast meadows of lush green grass and the shapeliest trees and bushes, and he could hear the ripple of running streams and the sweet twittering of myriads of birds. There was no sign of any man, so Diarmuid hurried on until, feeling a great thirst come over him, he knelt down by a crystal-clear spring and scooped up some water in his cupped hands. No sooner were his lips wet than he heard the sound of men tramping across the grass. But to his amazement, when he turned his head to look, there was nothing to be seen. A second time he tried to quench his thirst, and again he heard the same sound and again saw nothing. But the third time his eye caught sight of a jewelled drinking-horn lying just a few feet from him. 'I shall use this horn as a drinking-cup,' thought young Diarmuid, and this time he managed to drink a hornful of the refreshing water. And then he saw a very tall man in a cloak of dark crimson walking towards him. The colour of his cloak, Diarmuid could see as he drew nearer, matched that of his face, which was flushed and angry.

'Diarmuid O'Dyna!' cried the stranger. 'By what right do you come here to drink the water of my springs? Is there not enough in Erin to quench your miserable thirst?' And then he advanced on the young man with drawn sword. Diarmuid was not slow to meet him with his own sword and they fought the whole day long with neither getting the advantage. But just as the sun was setting, the stranger sprang into the water and disappeared completely. Diarmuid, astonished but exhausted and grateful for this respite, lay down on the grass and sank into a deep sleep. When he awoke at sunrise the dark stranger was standing beside him, his sword in hand. All the livelong day they fought again in fearsome combat and again at sunset the stranger vanished into the water in the same mysterious way. On the third day, however, just as the unknown warrior was about to spring into the water, Diarmuid threw his arms about him and they both sank into the water, locked in tight embrace.

Down and down they went, heavily but not too quickly, until their feet seemed to bump something very soft that burst like a bubble. A flood of morning light surrounded them and the stranger immediately wrenched himself away. Diarmuid felt far too weary to follow in pursuit, as he wished, and sank to the dry ground in a deep sleep.

He was awakened gently by the touch of a hand on his shoulder. He looked up and beheld a fair-haired young man holding a sword. As Diarmuid sprang up to unsheath his own sword, the young man merely smiled and replaced his own in his scabbard.

'Have no fear,' he said. 'I am your friend. This is a most dangerous spot for you to rest. Follow me and I shall find you somewhere safer.'

Diarmuid accompanied the handsome young stranger and presently they arrived at a kind of fortified castle, in front of which grew a profusion of multi-coloured fruit trees. They entered the main portal and passed through endless courtyards, halls and corridors, everyone respectfully clearing a path for them. The young man then ordered a bath, filled with perfumed herbs, to be prepared for Diarmuid, and when he had thoroughly refreshed himself in it, all his wounds were healed and all his weariness was gone. He was given a silken shirt, a mantle and a cloak to wear in place of his own torn raiment.

In answer to Diarmuid's many questions, the young man then explained: 'You are in the Land under the Sea and the warrior who battled with you by the spring is its King. I am his brother, and if you look at me very closely you will recognize me as the man who took service with Finn Mac Coole a short while ago.' As Diarmuid stared curiously at him, he saw him change imperceptibly into the massive, clumsy giant dragging the equally ugly, long-necked horse – and then, just as imperceptibly, back again into the fair-haired young man.

'Are you indeed the Giolla Dacker?' asked Diarmuid.

'Yes,' was the reply.

'And what has become of my Fenian companions who were carried off on that vile steed of yours?'

'Have no fear,' said the young man, smiling. 'They are safe, as you will see for yourself when we are gathered for the evening's feast. You and they, together with my own loyal men, are going to help me win back the rightful half of my kingdom, which my brother villainously seized on the death of my father. And when that is done successfully, you and your companions may ask for any reward that your hearts desire.'

Diarmuid and the prince shook hands and swore loyalty to each other.

Finn and his men had now been waiting for nearly five days for Diarmuid to return. Finally, Finn decided that they should attempt to climb up the island in search of him. They tied all the ropes in the ship together till they were long enough to reach the top of the island. Then Finn selected two of his men to climb up the sheer face of the cliff, taking the rope with them. Having reached the top, they tied one end to a ledge of rock, and then the rest of the Fenians climbed up after them. They set off along the path that Diarmuid himself had taken, but for some strange reason, never to be known, they arrived at another spot on the island, not by the spring but near a cave. Before settling down to rest there for the night, Finn decided to explore it to the very end in case of hidden dangers. But, amazingly, when they reached the end, it was bright dawn, although it had been sunset at the opening of the cave. And now, they too could see the fortified castle to which Diarmuid had been led by the prince. On a vast stretch of greensward in front of the main portal, warriors were fighting, in sport, with sword and spear, among them Diarmuid and the other men who had been carried off by the giant's horse. They caught sight of Finn and their Fenian companions and with a sky-rending shout of triumph ran out to meet them.

The prince greeted them warmly and repeated what he had already told Diarmuid. Finn and his band shook hands in turn with him and swore their loyalty in the battle which was to come.

Next morning the prince's men and the Fenians marched out to face the King's army, which had at least four times as many soldiers. But each single Fenian champion was three times as valorous as any of the enemy. Finn threw his spear up into the air, and shouted the Fenian war-cry and the two lines of battle rushed furiously towards each other. Amid the deafening clash of shields and swords every inch of ground was fiercely contested and all day long they fought without either side gaining the advantage. By sunset Finn could see that in time, unless something unexpected happened, the King's superiority in numbers would be decisive. So taking in a mighty breath he raised such a fearful war-cry that the earth trembled and young Diarmuid O'Dyna dashed forward as one inspired. Such was his speed and impetus that he cut right through the enemy lines and thus cleared a path for his comrades to follow. The King's men, taken aback by this sudden and irresistible onslaught, broke their ranks and began to flee in utter disorder. The

King himself was slain and the battle came to an end.

There was great feasting to celebrate the victory, after which the prince asked the Fenians to name their reward.

'As you did not insist upon your wages at the end of your service with me,' said Finn with a twinkle in his eye. 'I shall set my payments against yours and ask for nothing.' But the men who had been carried off on horseback in such humiliating fashion were not so easily satisfied. They protested and complained, and so finally they were allowed to choose their reward. Nothing would satisfy them but that fifteen of the prince's finest warriors should be mounted on the horse's back and the prince himself should grip the tail and return to Erin under the water, in exactly the same manner as they themselves had been taken from there.

'That demand is perfectly justified,' said the prince. 'If you go back to that selfsame spot where you first saw the Giolla Dacker, you may shortly expect to see us there, conveyed in the fashion you have decided on.'

And so the Fenians made their way back through the seemingly endless cave and then down the rope to their waiting boat. Before long they could see the unbeautiful horse with the fifteen warriors on his back and the hideous Giolla Dacker clutching his tail. As they alighted, very stiffly, one after the other, they were greeted with peals of uncontrollable laughter from Finn's men. Finn himself took no part in the mockery and tried to make his men show some sort of courtesy.

But before he had time to put out out his hand to greet the Giolla Dacker, the latter had vanished. Nor was there any sign of the fifteen warriors nor of the clumsy long-necked horse.

And that was the last Finn and his men ever saw of them.

STEPHEN CORRIN

Orpheus and Eurydice

The *Iliad* is a poem which tells of the siege of Troy and the exploits of Hector and Achilles. It is supposed to have been composed by the blind Homer. But long before the time of Homer there was another great poet and singer, Orpheus, around whose name innumerable myths and legends have been woven.

Orpheus was the son of Oeagrus, King of Thrace, and Calliope, one of the Nine Muses, who inspired poets. Apollo, the god of music and poetry, gave Orpheus a golden lyre and with this he would go to quiet, lonely places and play. But he was never left alone for long. Ants and spiders and bees would stop their work and come near to listen to him. Birds stopped singing and building their nests and perched on any twig they could find, transfixed by the beautiful sound of his playing. Wild beasts heard him from afar and would gather round to listen, but the smaller creatures had nothing to fear from them while Orpheus's music filled the air: their savage breasts were tamed. Not even the trees, the rocks and the mountains could resist the power of his music, and they would uproot themselves to come and join the magic circle of creatures, great and small, that had gathered around the god-inspired musician.

When the Argonauts went to Colchis in quest of the Golden Fleece, Orpheus accompanied them and it was his enchanted music which saved his companions from being lured to death by the singing Sirens on whose island countless sailors had perished. It was the golden strains of Orpheus's lyre that lulled to sleep the guardian dragon of the Fleece itself.

The nymphs in the valleys admired Orpheus, and the most beautiful of them, Eurydice, fell deeply in love with him and became his wife. For a while they lived together in the greatest harmony and bliss, for never were the bonds of love so strong as those which bound these two together, but one day Eurydice trod on a poisonous snake and was bitten in the ankle. She died almost immediately and descended to the underworld of Hades. Orpheus's grief was long and bitter and he would not be comforted. At last he begged Zeus, the greatest of the gods, for permission to descend to the underworld so that he might try to persuade Pluto, who was the ruler there, to release his beloved Eurydice and let her return again to the land of the living.

Zeus saw how deep was the suffering of Orpheus, so he granted him the right to descend to the darkness of the underworld to seek out his beloved. He had first to cross the River Styx, which flows down in a mighty sweep from a great rock and connects the upper to the nether world. At first the ferryman, Charon, stubbornly refused to transport him but when he heard the sweet music of Orpheus's lyre he was in such a state of wonderment that he yielded and ferried the musician across. Even more difficult an obstacle was the three-headed dog Cerberus, who guarded the gate at the entry to the underworld. His ferocious barking made the music of the lyre quite inaudible, but finally its melodious strains penetrated the ears of even that monstrous creature and Orpheus was allowed to pass through. Nor did his music fail to cast a spell on the Furies, who cast aside their whips and were silent as Orpheus passed them. The final barrier to Hades was the Pool of Memory, which one could not cross without knowing the password. However, this was willingly revealed to him by Persephone, Queen of the Underworld, who was bewitched by the sound of Orpheus's lyre.

In the Underworld itself the tortures of the victims were interrupted so that all, even the torturers, could enjoy Orpheus's sweet music. The ever-rotating wheel, to which Ixion was tied for his treachery to the gods, stood still for the first time. Tantalus, who had tried to trick the gods by offering his son's crooked body as part of a feast to them and whose punishment was to stand in the middle of a lake surrounded by luscious fruit-trees but never to satisfy his thirst or hunger, was for a while allowed to eat and drink. And Sisyphus, another trickster who had angered the gods, had some respite from the downward-rolling stone which it was his punishment to keep for ever pushing upward.

Then Orpheus had to appear before the dread Pluto himself. On his knees, with tears flowing from his eyes, he implored him to restore his beloved Eurydice to the land of the living, for life without her was unbearable torment. When Pluto refused, Orpheus took up his lyre and played such heart-rending music that even the fearsome ruler of the underworld was softened. Pluto agreed to restore Eurydice to life – but on one condition, namely, that Orpheus must not once look back as his beloved followed behind him, until she had safely reached the light of the living world. The gratitude of the stricken lover knew no bounds and he agreed without hesitation to what seemed to be a very simple condition. He began his journey back to the upper world and looked straight ahead of him. On and on he went,

hastening to complete his dangerous passage through Hades but . . . just as he was nearing the end, a dreadful suspicion suddenly overwhelmed him. Was Eurydice really following behind him (for he could hear no footsteps) or was Pluto playing some vile trick upon him? Orpheus looked fearfully back . . . only to hear the agonized cry of pain from Eurydice as she disappeared for ever from his sight.

Filled with rage and grief, Orpheus returned to the upper world and lived for many weeks without food or drink by the banks of the River Strymon, not caring what happened to him. He refused to worship the new god of wine, Dionysus, and so, to punish him, Dionysus ordered his wild followers, the Maenads, to tear him to pieces. They cut off Orpheus's head and threw it into the river.

The Nine Muses gathered up the remains of the greatest of all musicians and buried them at the foot of Mount Olympus. It was said that as his head floated down the river it still cried out the name of his beloved Eurydice and in the distance his golden lyre could be heard playing still.

JOAN AIKEN

All You've Ever Wanted

Matilda, you will agree, was a most unfortunate child. Not only had she three names each worse than the others – Matilda, Eliza and Agatha – but her father and mother died shortly after she was born, and she was brought up exclusively by her six aunts. These were all energetic women, and so on Monday Matilda was taught Algebra and Arithmetic by her Aunt Aggie, on Tuesday, Biology by her Aunt Beattie, on Wednesday Classics by her Aunt Cissie, on Thursday Dancing and Deportment by her Aunt Dorrie, on Friday Essentials by her Aunt Effie, and on Saturday French by her Aunt Florrie. Friday was the most alarming day, as Matilda never knew beforehand what Aunt Effie would decide on as the day's Essentials – sometimes it was cooking, or revolver practice, or washing, or boiler-making ('For you never know what a girl may need nowadays' as Aunt Effie rightly observed).

So that by Sunday, Matilda was often worn out, and thanked her stars that her seventh aunt, Gertie, had left for foreign parts many years before, and never threatened to come back and teach her Geology or Grammar on the only day when she was able to do as she liked.

However, poor Matilda was not entirely free from her Aunt Gertie, for on her seventh birthday, and each one after it, she received a little poem wishing her well, written on pink paper, decorated with silver flowers, and signed 'Gertrude Isabel Jones, to her niece, with much affection'. And the terrible disadvantage of the poems, pretty though they were, was that the wishes in them invariably came true. For instance the one on her eighth birthday read:

> *Now you are eight Matilda dear*
> *May shining gifts your place adorn*
> *And each day through the coming year*
> *Awake you with a rosy morn.*

The shining gifts were all very well – they consisted of a torch, a luminous watch, pins, needles, a steel soapbox, and a useful little silver brooch which said 'Matilda' in case she ever forgot her name – but the rosy morns were a great mistake. As you know, a red sky in the morning is the shepherd's warning, and the fatal result of Aunt Gertie's well-meaning verse was that it rained every day for the entire year.

Another   one   read:

> *Each morning make another friend*
> *Who'll be with you till light doth end,*
> *Cheery and frolicsome and gay,*
> *To pass the sunny hours away.*

For the rest of her life Matilda was overwhelmed by the number of friends she made in the course of that year – three hundred and sixty-five of them. Every morning she found another of them, anxious to cheer her and frolic with her, and the aunts complained that her lessons were being constantly interrupted. The worst of it was that she did not really like all the friends – some of them were so *very* cheery and frolicsome, and insisted on pillow-fights when she had a toothache, or sometimes twenty-one of them would get together and make her play hockey, which she hated. She was not even consoled by the fact that all her hours were sunny, because she was so busy in passing them away that she had no time to enjoy them.

> *Long miles and weary though you stray*
> *Your friends are never far away,*
> *And every day though you may roam,*
> *Yet night will find you back at home*

was another inconvenient wish. Matilda found herself forced to go for long, tiresome walks in all weathers, and it was no comfort to know that her friends were never far away, for although they often passed her on bicycles or in cars, they never gave her lifts.

However, as she grew older, the poems became less troublesome, and she began to enjoy bluebirds twittering in the garden, and endless vases of roses on her window-sill. Nobody knew where Aunt Gertie lived, and she never put in an address with her birthday greetings. It was therefore impossible to write and thank her for her varied good wishes, or hint that they might have been more carefully worded. But Matilda looked forward to meeting her one day, and thought she must be a most interesting person.

'You never knew what Gertrude would be up to next,' said Aunt Cissie. 'She was a thoughtless girl, and got into endless scrapes. But I will say this for her, she was very good-hearted.'

When Matilda was nineteen she took a job in the Ministry of Alarm and Despondency, a very cheerful place where, instead of typewriter ribbon, they used red tape, and there was a large laundry basket near the main entrance labelled The Usual Channels where all the letters were put which people did not want to answer themselves. Once every three months the letters were re-sorted and dealt out afresh to different people.

Matilda got on very well here and was perfectly happy. She went to see her six aunts on Sundays, and had almost forgotten the seventh by the time that her twentieth birthday had arrived. Her aunt, however, had not forgotten.

On the morning of her birthday Matilda woke very late, and had to rush off to work cramming her letters unopened into her pocket, to be read later on in the morning. She had no time to read them until ten minutes to eleven, but that, she told herself, was as it should be, since, as she had been born at eleven in the morning, her birthday did not really begin till then.

Most of the letters were from her 365 friends, but the usual pink and silver envelope was there, and she opened it with the usual feeling of slight uncertainty.

> *May all your leisure hours be blest,*
> *Your work prove full of interest,*
> *Your life hold many happy hours*
> *And all your way be strewn with flowers*

said the pink and silver slip in her fingers. 'From your affectionate Aunt Gertrude.'

Matilda was still pondering when a gong sounded in the passage outside. This was the signal for everyone to leave their work and dash down the passage to a trolley which sold them buns and coffee. Matilda left her let-

ters and dashed with the rest. Sipping her coffee and gossiping with her friends, she had forgotten the poem, when the voice of the Minister of Alarm and Despondency himself came down the corridor.

'What is all this? What does this mean?' he was saying.

The group round the trolley turned to see what he was talking about. And then Matilda flushed scarlet and spilt some of her coffee on the floor. For all along the respectable brown carpeting of the passage were growing flowers in the most riotous profusions – daisies, campanulas, crocuses, mimosa, foxgloves, tulips and lotuses. In some places the passage looked more like a jungle than anything else. Out of this jungle the little red-faced figure of the Minister fought its way.

'Who did it?' he said. But nobody answered.

Matilda went quietly away from the chattering group and pushed through the vegetation to her room, leaving a trail of buttercups and rhododendrons across the floor to her desk.

'I can't keep this quiet,' she thought desperately. And she was quite right. Mr Willoughby, who presided over the General Gloom Division, noticed almost immediately that when his secretary came into his room, there was something unusual about her.

'Miss Jones,' he said, 'I don't like to be personal, but have you noticed that wherever you go, you leave a trail of mixed flowers?'

Poor Matilda burst into tears.

'I know, I don't know *what* to do about it,' she sobbed.

Mr Willoughby was not used to secretaries who

burst into tears, let alone ones who left lobelias, prim-
roses and the rarer forms of cactus behind them when
they entered the room.

'It's very pretty,' he said. 'But not very practical.
Already it's almost impossible to get along the passage,
and I shudder to think what this room will be like when
these have grown a bit higher. I really don't think you
can go on with it, Miss Jones.'

'You don't think I do it on purpose, do you?' said
Matilda sniffing into her handkerchief. 'I can't stop it.
They just keep on coming.'

'In that case I am afraid,' replied Mr Willoughby,
'that you will not be able to keep on coming. We really
cannot have the Minstry overgrown in this way. I shall
be very sorry to lose you, Miss Jones. You have been
most efficient. What caused this unfortunate disability,
may I ask?'

'It's a kind of spell,' Matilda said, shaking the damp
out of her handkerchief on to a fine polyanthus.

'But my dear girl,' Mr Willoughby exclaimed testily,
'you have a National Magic Insurance card, haven't
you? Good heavens – why don't you go to the Public
Magician?'

'I never thought of that,' she confessed. 'I'll go at
lunchtime.'

Fortunately for Matilda the Public Magician's office
lay just across the square from where she worked, so
that she did not cause too much disturbance, though
the Borough Council could never account for the rare
and exotic flowers which suddenly sprang up in the
middle of their dusty lawns.

The Public Magician received her briskly, examined her with an occultiscope, and asked her to state particulars of her trouble.

'It's a spell,' said Matilda, looking down at a pink Christmas rose growing unseasonably beside her chair.

'In that case we can soon help you. Fill in that form, *if* you please.' He pushed a printed slip at her across the table.

It said: 'To be filled in by persons suffering from spells, incantations, philtres, Evil Eye, etc.'

Matilda filled in name and address of patient, nature of spell, and date, but when she came to name and address of person by whom spell was cast, she paused.

'I don't know her address,' she said.

'Then I'm afraid you'll have to find it. Can't do anything without an address,' the Public Magician replied.

Matilda went out into the street very disheartened. The Public Magician could do nothing better than advise her to put an advertisement into *The Times* and the *International Sorcerers' Bulletin*, which she accordingly did:

AUNT GERTRUDE PLEASE COMMUNICATE MATILDA MUCH DISTRESSED BY LAST POEM.

While she was in the Post Office sending off her advertisements (and causing a good deal of confusion by the number of forget-me-nots she left about), she wrote and posted her resignation to Mr Willoughby, and then went sadly to the nearest Underground Station.

'Aintcher left something behind?' a man said to her at the top of the escalator. She looked back at the trail of daffodils across the station entrance and hurried anxiously down the stairs. As she ran round a corner at the bottom angry shouts told her that blooming lilies had interfered with the works and the escalator had stopped.

She tried to hide in the gloom at the far end of the platform, but a furious station official found her.

'Wotcher mean by it?' he said, shaking her elbow. 'It'll take three days to put the station right, and look at my platform!'

The stone slabs were split and pushed aside by vast peonies, which kept growing, and threatened to block the line.

'It isn't my fault – really it isn't,' poor Matilda stammered.

'The company can sue you for this, you know,' he began, when a train came in. Pushing past him, she squeezed into the nearest door.

She began to thank her stars for the escape, but it was too soon. A powerful and penetrating smell of onions rose round her feet where the white flowers of wild garlic had sprung.

When Aunt Gertie finally read the advertisement in a ten-months' old copy of the *International Sorcerers' Bulletin,* she packed her luggage and took the next aeroplane back to England. For she was still just as Aunt Cissie had described her – thoughtless, but very good-hearted.

'Where is the poor child?' she asked Aunt Aggie.

'I should say she was poor,' her sister replied tartly. 'It's a pity you didn't come home before, instead of making her life a misery for twelve years. You'll find her out in the summerhouse.'

Matilda had been living out there ever since she left the Ministry of Alarm and Despondency, because her aunts kindly but firmly, and quite reasonably, said that they could not have the house filled with vegetation.

She had an axe, with which she cut down the worst growths every evening, and for the rest of the time she kept as still as she could, and earned some money by doing odd jobs of typing and sewing.

'My poor dear child,' Aunt Gertie said breathlessly. 'I had no idea that my little verses would have this effect. What ever shall we do?'

'Please do something,' Matilda implored her, sniffing. This time it was not tears, but a cold she had caught from living in perpetual draughts.

'My dear, there isn't anything I can do. It's bound to last till the end of the year – that sort of spell is completely unalterable.'

'Well, at least can you stop sending me the verses?' asked Matilda. 'I don't want to sound ungrateful . . .'

'Even that I can't do,' her aunt said gloomily. 'It's a banker's order at the Magician's Bank. Once a year from seven to twenty-one. Oh, dear, I thought it would be such *fun* for you. At least you only have one more, though.'

'Yes, but heaven knows what that'll be.' Matilda sneezed despondently and put another sheet of paper into her typewriter. There seemed to be nothing to do but wait. However, they did decide that it might be a good thing to go and see the Public Magician on the morning of Matilda's twenty-first birthday.

Aunt Gertie paid the taxi-driver and tipped him heavily not to grumble about the mass of delphiniums sprouting out of the mat of his cab.

'Good heavens, if it isn't Gertude Jones!' the Public Magician exclaimed. 'Haven't seen you since we were at college together. How are you? Same old irresponsible Gertie? Remember that hospital you endowed with endless beds and the trouble it caused? And the row with the cigarette manufacturers over the extra million boxes of cigarettes for the soldiers?'

When the situation was explained to him he laughed heartily.

'Just like you, Gertie. Well-meaning isn't the word.'

At eleven promptly, Matilda opened her pink envelope.

> *Matilda, now you're twenty-one*
> *May you have every sort of fun;*
> *May you have all you've ever wanted,*
> *And every future wish be granted.*

'Every future wish be granted – then I wish Aunt Gertie would lose her power of wishing,' cried Matilda; and immediately Aunt Gertie did.

But as Aunt Gertie with her usual thoughtlessness had said, 'May you have all you've *ever wanted*' Matilda had quite a lot of rather inconvenient things to dispose of, including a lion cub and a baby hippopotamus.

STEPHEN CORRIN

Odysseus and Circe

When the Greeks went to war against the Trojans to try to recapture the divinely beautiful Helen, who had been stolen from her husband Menelaus by Paris, the son of Priam, King of Troy, Odysseus was one of the many great warriors in their ranks. And when the Greeks were finally the victors, thanks mainly to the cunning device of the Wooden Horse which Odysseus had thought of, most of them sailed back home in their long ships, weary and homesick after their ten long years of battle.

Odysseus was not allowed a safe return home because he angered Poseidon, god of the seas, by killing his son Polyphemus, the hideous man-eating Cyclops. Poseidon played all sorts of tricks on Odysseus to hinder him, and his many adventures are related by Homer in his great epic poem the *Odyssey*.

One of these adventures was with the enchantress Circe.

One morning, weary with day after day of hard rowing under a mercilessly blazing sun, Odysseus and his men arrived at the island of Aeaea. Too tired even to land, they all went to sleep and did not wake up for two whole days. As they were short of provisions, Odysseus decided to go and explore the island to see what it offered in the way of food and shelter. He found any number of streams of fresh water and many stretches of fragrant woods and, most important of all, a long column of bluish smoke rising from somewhere in the middle of the island. Back he went to his men and reported what he had found, but having already survived so many perilous situations the men decided it would not be wise for all of them to go ashore. Odysseus agreed that the crew should be divided into two parties, each with a leader, and that one party should stay behind to guard their only remaining ship. Then they drew lots as to which one should go on land. The lot fell to Eurylochus, a friend of Odysseus, and so he, with twenty-two rather unwilling companions, went ashore and made straight for the direction of the column of blue smoke.

Eventually they came to a clearing in the midst of which stood a magnificent palace of gleaming white marble, and as they drew nearer a band of wild beasts, lions, tigers, wolves and bears, came running towards them. The men stood rooted to the spot, petrified with fear, expecting to be torn to pieces immediately. But to their great relief and amazement these apparently savage beasts behaved just like affectionate dogs, rubbing themselves against the men and wagging their tails. So they plucked up courage and walked through the marble pillars into the palace itself. Now they could hear the sound of sweet singing and the whirr of a loom and they called out a greeting to announce their presence. Presently two great polished doors opened wide and a tall woman appeared, smiling invitingly. This was the sorceress, Circe. Eurylochus felt in his bones that there was some kind of trap awaiting them and he refused Circe's invitation to partake of food and drink, but all the other men, faint and famished as they were, accepted eagerly. Eurylochus managed to slip away and hide in a spot from where he could watch what was happening without being seen. He saw Circe lead the men into a stately hall and seat them at a table laden with tempting bowls of mouth-watering food, into which four fair maidens poured wine and honey and a sort of barley-meal. The men ate and drank greedily, for not a morsel of food had passed their lips for several days, let alone such luxurious fare. Eurylochus looked on hungrily, hardly able to resist rushing forward and grabbing something to stuff into his parched mouth. Then he saw Circe walk round the table behind the men and strike each one lightly with a wand. And lo and behold! the men's heads turned instantly into pigs' heads, their bodies into pigs' bodies and they dropped from their benches on all fours and grunted and snorted like swine. Then she shooed them out of the stately hall and ushered them unceremoniously into pigsties where she threw them handfuls of acorns and beech nuts.

Eurylochus, thankful that he had escaped this terrible transformation, slipped quietly from his hiding place and returned to the ship to report these sad happenings to Odysseus. The wily warrior immediately took up his great bow and sword and, despite all Eurylochus's earnest pleadings, made him lead the way back to Circe's palace. But half way there Eurylochus

became so frightened that Odysseus allowed him to return to the ship and went on alone, determined to confront the sorceress and force her to restore his men to their human shape. But how? Fortunately for him, the god Hermes suddenly appeared in his path in the form of a handsome young man, wearing winged sandals and carrying a golden wand.

Odysseus was about to walk past him, so eager was he to hasten to the aid of his men, when the god spoke.

'I know, Odysseus, that you are on your way to the palace of the enchantress Circe, but I fear that without my help you will be of little service to your companions in their pigsties. And do you too wish to be changed into a pig?'

Odysseus was so startled to find that the stranger knew so much about his plight that he paused to listen further.

'You must do as I instruct you,' continued Hermes, and he handed Odysseus a milk-white flower with a black root which he plucked from below an oak tree. 'Take this,' he said, 'and guard it carefully, for it has powers far stronger than those possessed by Circe. As long as you have this plant in your possession, none of her spells can harm you. Her wine will not transform you into an animal, her sword cannot wound you nor her wand enchant you. And when she sees that she is powerless to do anything to you, you can compel her to restore your companions to their human form. But I must warn you that she will do all she can to charm you into staying in her palace until she can find an opportunity to rob you of your courage. Do not be beguiled!' And with those words the messenger of the gods winged his way into the blue sky.

Odysseus now walked into the palace and was warmly welcomed by the smiling Circe. She treated him with great honour, led him to a golden seat and offered him wine in a golden cup. As soon as he had drunk it, Circe's expression changed. She struck Odysseus lightly with her wand and cried out, 'Now go and join your friends in the pigsties!' To her disappointment and surprise, however, no change came over Odysseus. He sprang nimbly from his golden chair and drew his sword as if to attack her. Circe fell to the ground, clasped Odysseus round the knees and pleaded for her life.

'I do not know what manner of mortal man you are,' she cried. 'No human being has ever before withstood my spells. Only the renowned Odysseus, wisest of all men, could have resisted me thus . . . but perhaps you are indeed Odysseus!'

'I am he,' replied the warrior sternly, 'and I will spare your life if you restore my men to their human shape and solemnly swear never again to use your evil spells against us!'

The sorceress rose to her feet and once again she was all sweetness. She placed her hand upon the warrior's sword and swore that never more would she plan mischief against him or his companions. She then ordered a bath to be prepared for him, and when he had refreshed himself in the sweet-scented waters her attendants arrayed him in a fresh cloak and tunic and led him into a splendid banqueting hall, where a great feast had been prepared in his honour. But Odysseus refused to partake of anything until all his men had joined him at the table. Within a few seconds they came in, newly bathed, clad in fresh robes, and glad to see their leader safe and sound. Then Circe confessed to them that the god Hermes had told her that Odysseus would indeed visit her island on his journey home from Troy and she drank a toast to their eternal friendship.

When the feast was over Odysseus went back to his ship and told the men who had been guarding it everything that had taken place on the island. He led them back to Circe's palace, where they were joyfully reunited with their companions.

They were treated royally by the enchantress (for she never broke her oath) and were invited to stay for a whole year.

Towards the end of that time, however, the men became homesick and longed to see their families and wives again. Circe warned them that they would meet with many dangerous adventures on their journey homewards and gave them valuable advice on how to behave in face of them. Most important of all she gave them a wind which would carry them safely past the island of the Sirens, those lovely sea-maidens whose songs lure men to certain death.

And so finally they left.

One day when a most unusual calm lay over the seas, they espied a wonderful island from which they seemed to catch the sound of almost heavenly singing. Odysseus knew at once that the singers were those very Sirens about whom Circe had warned them. He ordered his men to put wax pellets in their ears so that they would be deaf to the alluring music and commanded them to tie him to the mast of the ship so that he himself would be able to enjoy the singing without being bewitched and thus tempted to throw himself into the waves. But once he was securely tied, the music seemed more lovely and seductive than ever and the temptation became so great that he struggled as one mad to break free and pleaded with his men to untie him. It was indeed a pitiful and agonizing sight to see so mighty a warrior thus weakened and his men were almost ready to obey him. But Eurylochus stopped them, and ordered them to make Odysseus's bonds all the tighter. And so, though straining every sinew to detach himself from his self-imposed fetters, Odysseus was held secure until the ship was steered past the perilous island and the Sirens' song could no longer be heard. Then the men unfastened their leader's bonds and took the pellets out of their ears, and their tremendous shout of triumph echoed far over the waves.

At long last, and after many further adventures, Odysseus returned to his home, there to face the most daunting task of all, and one that required all his superhuman cunning, before he could win back his ever-faithful wife Penelope and his brave son Telemachus.

During Odysseus's many long years of absence, scores of suitors had come to seek the hand of Penelope and on their visits to her home had used it and everything in it as though they were lords and masters there.

Odysseus was determined to punish them. He disguised himself as a beggar and together with his faithful swineherd Eumaeus and Telemachus (to whom he had made himself known) he went to his home, where his dog Argus recognized him.

Penelope had promised to marry the man who shot best with the bow of Odysseus. But not one of the suitors could even bend the bow. Odysseus himself then took it and attacked them and, supported by his son, he vanquished them one after the other.

Reunited at last with his wife and son, Odysseus, most illustrious among warriors, lived to a happy old age.

JACK LONDON

The Love Master

As White Fang watched Weedon Scott approach, he
bristled and snarled to advertise that he would not
submit to punishment. Twenty-four hours had passed
since he had slashed open the hand that was now ban-
daged and held up by a sling to keep the blood out of
it. In the past White Fang had experienced delayed
punishments, and he apprehended that such a one
was about to befall him. How could it be otherwise? He
had committed what was to him sacrilege – sunk his
fangs into the holy flesh of a god, and of a superior-
looking god at that. In the nature of things, and of
intercourse with gods, something terrible awaited
him.

The god sat down several feet away. White Fang
could see nothing dangerous in that. When the gods
administered punishment they stood on their legs.
Besides, this god had no club, no whip, no fire-arm.
And furthermore, he himself was free. No chain nor
stick bound him. He could escape into safety while the
god was scrambling to his feet. In the meantime he
would wait and see.

The god remained quiet, made no movement; and
White Fang's snarl slowly dwindled to a growl that

ebbed down in his throat and ceased. Then the god spoke, and at the first sound of his voice the hair rose on White Fang's neck and the growl rushed up in his throat. But the god made no hostile movement, and went on calmly talking. For a time White Fang growled in unison with him, a correspondence of rhythm being established between growl and voice. But the god talked on interminably. He talked to White Fang as White Fang had never been talked to before. He talked softly and soothingly, with a gentleness that somehow, somewhere, touched White Fang. In spite of himself and all the pricking warnings of his instinct, White Fang began to have confidence in this god. He had a feeling of security that was belied by all his experience with men.

After a long time the god got up and went into the cabin. White Fang scanned him apprehensively when he came out. He had neither whip nor club nor weapon. Nor was his uninjured hand behind his back hiding something. He sat down as before, in the same spot, several feet away. He held out a small piece of meat. White Fang pricked his ears and investigated it suspiciously, managing to look at the same time both at the meat and the god, alert for any overt act, his body tense and ready to spring away at the first sign of hostility.

Still the punishment delayed. The god merely held near to his nose a piece of meat. And about the meat there seemed nothing wrong. Still White Fang suspected; and though the meat was proffered to him with short inviting thrusts of the hand, he refused to touch it. The gods were all-wise, and there was no telling what masterful treachery lurked behind that apparently harmless piece of meat. In past experience, especially in dealing with squaws, meat and punishment had often been disastrously related.

In the end, the god tossed the meat on the snow at White Fang's feet. He smelled the meat carefully, but he did not look at it. While he smelled it he kept his eyes on the god. Nothing happened. He took the meat into his mouth and swallowed it. Still nothing happened. The god was actually offering him another piece of meat. Again he refused to take it from the hand, and again it was tossed to him. This was repeated a number of times, but there came a time when the god refused to toss it. He kept it in his hand and steadfastly proffered it.

The meat was good meat, and White Fang was hungry. Bit by bit, infinitely cautious, he approached the hand. At last the time came that he decided to eat the meat from the hand. He never took his eyes from the god, thrusting his head forward with ears flattened back and hair involuntarily rising and cresting on his neck. Also a low growl rumbled in his throat as warning that he was not to be trifled with. He ate the meat, and nothing happened. Piece by piece he ate all the meat, and nothing happened. Still the punishment delayed.

He licked his chops and waited. The god went on talking. In his voice there was kindness – something of which White Fang had no experience whatever. And within him it aroused feelings which he had likewise never experienced before. He was aware of a certain strange satisfaction, as though some need were being gratified, as though some void in his being were being filled. Then again came the prod of his instinct and the warning of past experience. The gods were ever crafty, and they had unguessed ways of attaining their ends.

Ah, he had thought so! There it came now, the god's hand, cunning to hurt, thrusting out to him, descending upon his head. But the god went on talking. His voice was soft and soothing. In spite of the menacing hand the voice inspired confidence. And in spite of the assuring voice the hand inspired distrust. White Fang was torn by conflicting feelings, impulses. It seemed he would fly to pieces, so terrible was the control he was exerting, holding together by an unwonted

decision the counter-forces that struggled within him for mastery.

He compromised. He snarled and bristled and flattened his ears. But he neither snapped nor sprang away. The hand descended. Nearer and nearer it came. It touched the ends of his upstanding hair. He shrank down under it. It followed down after him, pressing more closely against him. Shrinking, almost shivering, he still managed to hold himself together. It was a torment, this hand that touched him and violated his instinct. He could not forget in a day all the evil that had been wrought him at the hands of men. But it was the will of the god, and he strove to submit.

The hand lifted and descended again in a patting, caressing movement. This continued, but every time the hand lifted the hair lifted under it. And every time the hand descended the ears flattened down and a cavernous growl surged in his throat. White Fang growled and growled with insistent warning. By this means he announced that he was prepared to retaliate for any hurt he might receive. There was no telling when the god's ulterior motive might be disclosed. At any moment that soft, confidence-inspiring voice might break forth in a roar of wrath, that gentle and caressing hand transform itself into a vice-like grip to hold him helpless and administer punishment.

But the god talked on softly, and ever the hand rose and fell with non-hostile pats. White Fang experienced dual feelings. It was distasteful to his instinct. It restrained him, opposed the will of him towards personal liberty. And yet it was not physically painful. On the contrary, it was even pleasant, in a physical way. The patting movement slowly and carefully changed to a rubbing of the ears about their bases, and the physical pleasure even increased a little. Yet he continued to fear, and he stood on guard, expectant of unguessed evil, alternately suffering and enjoying as one feeling or the other came uppermost and swayed him.

'Well, I'll be gosh-swoggled!'

So spoke Matt, coming out of the cabin, his sleeves rolled up, a pan of dirty dish-water in his hands, arrested in the act of emptying the pan by the sight of Weedon Scott patting White Fang.

At the instant his voice broke the silence White Fang leaped back, snarling savagely at him.

Matt regarded his employer with grieved disapproval.

'If you don't mind my expressin' my feelin's, Mr Scott, I'll make free to say you're seventeen kinds of a damn fool, an' all of 'em different, an' then some.'

Weedon Scott smiled with a superior air, gained his feet, and walked over to White Fang. He talked soothingly to him, but not for long, then slowly put out his hand, rested it on White Fang's head, and resumed the interrupted patting. White Fang endured it, keeping his eyes fixed suspiciously, not upon the man that petted him, but upon the man that stood in the doorway.

'You may be number one tip-top minin' expert, all right, all right,' the dog-musher delivered himself oracularly, 'but you missed the chance of your life when you was a boy an' didn't run off an' join a circus.'

MR CORBETT'S GHOST
AND OTHER STORIES
Leon Garfield

Three chilling stories for those who like a shivery thrill.

SWEETS FROM A STRANGER
AND OTHER STRANGE TALES
Nicholas Fisk

A collection of imaginative and macabre science fiction stories.

MESSAGES
Marjorie Darke

A collection of shivery tales which you'd better not read alone . . .

IMAGINE THAT!
Sara and Stephen Corrin

Fifteen fantastic tales, mostly traditional, from all over the world, including China and Asia.

THE GHOSTS COMPANION
ed. Peter Haining

Thrilling ghost stories by well-known writers – and the incidents which first gave them the idea.

THE WILD RIDE
AND OTHER SCOTTISH STORIES
ed. Gordon Jarvie

A spirited anthology of modern short stories from Scotland, ranging widely through ghost stories, adventure, drama and humour.

GUARDIAN ANGELS
ed. Stephanie Nettell

An anthology of stories specially written to commemorate the prestigious *Guardian* Children's Book Award's 20th anniversary.

TALES FOR THE TELLING
Edna O'Brien

A collection of heroic Irish tales to stir the imagination.

THE GNOME FACTORY
AND OTHER STORIES
James Reeves

The imagination of James Reeves's stories and the wit of Edward Ardizzone's drawings combine to make this an enchanting collection.